ISAAC ASIMOV'S
ROBOT CITY™

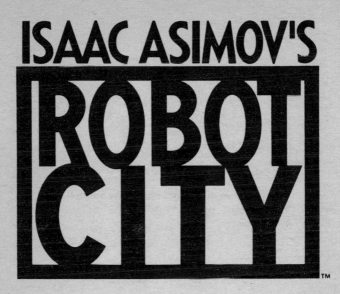

ISAAC ASIMOV'S ROBOT CITY ™

BOOK 3: CYBORG
WILLIAM F. WU

A Byron Preiss Visual Publications, Inc. Book

ACE BOOKS, NEW YORK

ISAAC ASIMOV'S ROBOT CITY
BOOK 3: CYBORG

An Ace Book/published by arrangement with
Byron Preiss Visual Publications, Inc.

PRINTING HISTORY
Ace edition/November 1987

Ace Books are published by The Berkley Publishing Group,
200 Madison Avenue, New York, New York 10016.
The name "Ace" and the "A" logo are
trademarks belonging to Charter Communications, Inc.
PRINTED IN THE UNITED STATES OF AMERICA

10 9 8 7 6 5 4 3 2 1

ACKNOWLEDGMENTS

Special thanks for help in writing this novel are due to David M. Harris, Michael P. Kube-McDowell, Rob Chilson, Alison Tellure, my parents, Dr. William Q. Wu and Cecile F. Wu, and Plus Five Computer Services, Inc.

This novel is dedicated to
Laura J. LeHew
who always remains very special

CONTENTS

CYBERNETIC ORGANISM
ISAAC ASIMOV

A robot is a robot and an organism is an organism.

An organism, as we all know, is built up of cells. From the molecular standpoint, its key molecules are nucleic acids and proteins. These float in a watery medium, and the whole has a bony support system. It is useless to go on with the description, since we are all familiar with organisms and since we are examples of them ourselves.

A robot, on the other hand, is (as usually pictured in science fiction) an object, more or less resembling a human being, constructed out of strong, rust-resistant metal. Science fiction writers are generally chary of describing the robotic details too closely since they are not usually essential to the story and the writers are generally at a loss how to do so.

The impression one gets from the stories, however, is that a robot is wired, so that it has wires through which electricity flows rather than tubes through which blood flows. The ultimate source of power is either unnamed, or is assumed to partake of the nature of nuclear power.

What of the robotic brain?

When I wrote my first few robot stories in 1939 and 1940, I imagined a "positronic brain" of a spongy type of platinum-iridium alloy. It was platinum-iridium because that is a particularly inert metal and is least likely to undergo chemical changes. It was spongy so that it would offer an enormous surface on which electrical patterns could be formed and un-formed. It was "positronic" because four years before my first robot story, the positron had been discovered as a reverse kind of electron, so that "positronic" in place of "electronic" had a delightful science-fiction sound.

Nowadays, of course, my positronic platinum-iridium brain is hopelessly archaic. Even ten years after its invention it became outmoded. By the end of the 1940s, we came to realize that a robot's brain must be a kind of computer. Indeed, if a robot were to be as complex as the robots in my most recent novels, the robot brain-computer must be every bit as complex as the human brain. It must be made of tiny microchips no larger than, and as complex as, brain cells.

But now let us try to imagine something that is neither organism nor robot, but a combination of the two. Perhaps we can think of it as an organism-robot or "orbot." That would clearly be a poor name, for it is only "robot" with the first two letters transposed. To say "orgabot", instead, is to be stuck with a rather ugly word.

We might call it a robot-organism, or a "robotanism", which, again, is ugly, or "roborg". To my ears, "roborg" doesn't sound bad, but we can't have that. Something else has arisen.

The science of computers was given the name "cybernetics" by Norbert Weiner a generation ago, so that if we consider something that is part robot and part organism and remember that a robot is cybernetic in nature, we might think of the mixture as a "cybernetic organism", or a "cyborg". In fact, that is the name that has stuck and is used.

To see what a cyborg might be, let's try starting with a human organism and moving toward a robot; and when we are quite done with that, let's start with a robot and move toward a human being.

To move from a human organism toward a robot, we must

begin replacing portions of the human organism with robotic parts. We already do that in some ways. For instance, a good percentage of the original material of my teeth is now metallic, and metal is, of course, the robotic substance *par excellence*.

The replacements don't have to be metallic, of course. Some parts of my teeth are now ceramic in nature, and can't be told at a glance from the natural dentine. Still, even though dentine is ceramic in appearance and even, to an extent, in chemical structure, it was originally laid down by living material and bears the marks of its origin. The ceramic that has replaced the dentine shows no trace of life, now or ever.

We can go further. My breastbone, which had to be split longitudinally in an operation a few years back, was for a time held together by metallic staples, which have remained in place ever since. My sister-in-law has an artificial hip-joint replacement. There are people who have artificial arms or legs and such non-living limbs are being designed, as time passes on, to be ever more complex and useful. There are people who have lived for days and even months with artificial hearts, and many more people who live for years with pacemakers.

We can imagine, little by little, this part and that part of the human being replaced by inorganic materials and engineering devices. Is there any part which we would find difficult to replace, even in imagination?

I don't think anyone would hesitate there. Replace every part of the human being but one—the limbs, the heart, the liver, the skeleton, and so on—and the product would remain human. It would be a human being with artificial parts, but it would be a human being.

But what about the brain?

Surely, if there is one thing that makes us human it is the brain. If there is one thing that makes us a human *individual*, it is the intensely complex makeup, the emotions, the learning, the memory content of our particular brain. You can't simply replace a brain with a thinking device off some factory shelf. You have to put in something that incorporates all that a natural brain has learned, that possesses all its memory, and that mimics its exact pattern of working.

An artificial limb might not work exactly like a natural one, but might still serve the purpose. The same might be true of an artificial lung, kidney, or liver. An artificial brain, however, must be the *precise* replica of the brain it replaces, or the human being in question is no longer the same human being.

It is the brain, then, that is the sticking point in going from human organism to robot.

And the reverse?

In my story "The Bicentennial Man", I described the passage of my robot-hero, Andrew Martin, from robot to man. Little by little, he had himself changed, till his every visible part was human in appearance. He displayed an intelligence that was increasingly equivalent (or even superior) to that of a man. He was an artist, a historian, a scientist, an administrator. He forced the passage of laws guaranteeing robotic rights, and achieved respect and admiration in the fullest degree.

Yet at no point could he make himself accepted as a *man*. The sticking point, here, too, was his robotic brain. He found that he had to deal with that before the final hurdle could be overcome.

Therefore, we come down to the dichotomy, body and brain. The ultimate cyborgs are those in which the body and brain don't match. That means we can have two classes of complete cyborgs:

a) a robotic brain in a human body, or
b) a human brain in a robotic body.

We can take it for granted that in estimating the worth of a human being (or a robot, for that matter) we judge first by superficial appearance.

I can very easily imagine a man seeing a woman of superlative beauty and gazing in awe and wonder at the sight. "What a beautiful woman," he will say, or think, and he could easily imagine himself in love with her on the spot. In romances, I believe that happens as a matter of routine. And, of course, a woman seeing a man of superlative beauty is surely likely to react in precisely the same way.

If you fall in love with a striking beauty, you are scarcely likely to spend much time asking if she (or he, of course) has any brains, or possesses a good character, or has good judgment or kindness or warmth. If you find out eventually that good looks are the person's only redeeming quality, you are liable to make excuses and continue to be guided, for a time at least, by the conditioned reflex of erotic response. Eventually, of course, you will tire of good looks without content, but who knows how long that will take?

On the other hand, a person with a large number of good qualities who happened to be distinctly plain might not be likely to entangle you in the first place unless you were intelligent enough to see those good qualities so that you might settle down to a lifetime of happiness.

What I am saying, then, is that a cyborg with a robotic brain in a human body is going to be accepted by most, if not all, people as a human being; while a cyborg with a human brain in a robotic body is going to be accepted by most, if not all, people as a robot. You are, after all—at least to most people—what you seem to be.

These two diametrically opposed cyborgs will not, however, pose a problem to human beings to the same degree.

Consider the robotic brain in the human body and ask why the transfer should be made. A robotic brain is better off in a robotic body since a human body is far the more fragile of the two. You might have a young and stalwart human body in which the brain has been damaged by trauma and disease, and you might think, "Why waste that magnificent human body? Let's put a robotic brain in it so that it can live out its life."

If you were to do that, the human being that resulted would not be the original. It would be a different individual human being. You would not be conserving an individual but merely a specific mindless body. And a human body, however fine, is (without the brain that goes with it) a cheap thing. Every day, half a million new bodies come into being. There is no need to save any one of them if the brain is done.

On the other hand, what about a human brain in a robotic body? A human brain doesn't last forever, but it can last up to ninety years without falling into total uselessness. It is not at all unknown to have a ninety-year-old who is still sharp, and capable of rational and worthwhile thought. And yet we also know that many a superlative mind has vanished after twenty or thirty years because the body that housed it (and was worthless in the absence of the mind) had become uninhabitable through trauma or disease. There would be a strong impulse then to transfer a perfectly good (even superior) brain into a robotic body to give it additional decades of useful life.

Thus, when we say "cyborg" we are very likely to think, just about exclusively, of a human brain in a robotic body—and we are going to think of that as a robot.

We might argue that a human mind is a human mind, and that it is the mind that counts and not the surrounding support mechanism, and we would be right. I'm sure that any rational court would decide that a human-brain cyborg would have all the legal rights of a man. He could vote, he could be enslaved, and so on.

And yet suppose a cyborg were challenged: "Prove that you have a human brain and not a robotic brain, before I let you have human rights."

The easiest way for a cyborg to offer the proof is for him to demonstrate that he is not bound by the Three Laws of Robotics. Since the Three Laws enforce socially acceptable behavior, this means he must demonstrate that he is capable of human (i.e. nasty) behavior. The simplest and most unanswerable argument is simply to knock the challenger down, breaking his jaw in the process, since no robot could do that. (In fact, in my story "Evidence", which appeared in 1947, I use this as a way of proving someone is not a robot—but in that case there was a catch.)

But if a cyborg must continually offer violence in order to prove he has a human brain, that will not necessarily win him friends.

For that matter, even if he is accepted as human and allowed to vote and to rent hotel rooms and do all the other things human beings can do, there must nevertheless be some regulations that distinguish between him and complete human beings. The cyborg would be stronger than a man, and his metallic fists could be viewed as lethal weapons. He might still be forbidden to strike a human being, even in self-defense. He couldn't engage in various sports on an equal basis with human beings, and so on.

Ah, but need a human brain be housed in a metallic robotic body? What about housing it in a body made of ceramic and plastic and fiber so that it looks and feels like a human body—and has a human brain besides?

But you know, I suspect that the cyborg will still have his troubles. He'll be *different*. No matter how small the difference is, people will seize upon it.

We know that people who have human brains and full human bodies sometimes hate each other because of a slight difference in skin pigmentation, or a slight variation in the shape of the nose, eyes, lips, or hair.

We know that people who show no difference in any of the physical characteristics that have come to represent a cause for hatred, may yet be at daggers-drawn over matters that are not physical at all, but cultural—differences in religion, or in political outlook, or in place of birth, or in language, or in just the accent of a language.

Let's face it. Cyborgs will have their difficulties, no matter what.

CHAPTER 1
THE KEY TO PERIHELION

Derec sighed and ran his hand through his brush-cut sandy hair. "Katherine, I don't know if this stupid computer knows who has the Key to Perihelion or not. Anyhow, if it does, it won't tell me. I've asked it every way I can think of." He swiveled his chair away from the computer console to face her.

Katherine looked down at him from where she stood, and shook her head in apparent disgust. "I didn't know *computers* could be stupid," she said pointedly.

"Well, this one is," he muttered lamely, feeling his face grow hot. "Look if someone else programmed a higher priority of secrecy into the computer, it won't answer any questions it was forbidden to answer. I can't do anything about that." He was glad he was seated. She was a bit taller than he, though he was—he hoped—still growing. He guessed that she was a year or two older than he was, but that was as uncertain as the rest of her identity . . . and his.

Derec sprang out of his chair to put some distance between them and started pacing around the room. Through his manipulation of the computer, he had ordered the builder robots of Robot City to continue developing the quarters he and Kather-

1

ine shared. They had constructed a bedroom for each of them, a kitchen area, and a console for the computer access equipment he had put together himself. Now he strode around the perimeter of the office, burning up nervous energy.

The apartment was hexagonal, and the furniture was shaped from the interior surface. Light glowed from the ceiling itself in a pleasant, soft diffusion. The room walls now obscured the elegant shape of the quarters, which resembled the interior of a crystal, but he and Katherine were more comfortable than before, and more independent.

Ever since Derec had stopped Robot City from its automatic, frantic, and self-destructive growth, they had been living in a city that almost resembled a normal one. Construction now continued at a steady pace, within the capacity of the city to adjust as it grew. With the Laws of Robotics in effect, the two humans had a comfortable and safe existence here now.

The First Law of Robotics is: "A robot may not injure a human being, or, through inaction, allow a human being to come to harm."

"Look, Derec," said Katherine. "We both want to get off this planet, I guess. At the moment, we aren't suffering here. Sure, if we had a ship, we'd be gone by now. But as long as that Key is our only chance to get away, we simply have to find it."

Her tone was milder now, Derec noticed, but he just spun around, turning his back on her, and went on pacing. Ever since he had found out that she was not really Katherine Ariel Burgess, as she had told him she was, he had known he could not trust her. Or, at least, he could only believe her when she was being sarcastic or condescending. When she sounded pleasant, he had to figure out what she was up to.

Besides, he still suffered from his amnesia. It was a little too awkward to demand her identity when he couldn't even figure out his own. In fact, even raising the subject was embarrassing. The situation left him perpetually uneasy. The best place to get away from it was in the computer.

He moved past her and threw himself back into the chair. Then he started working on the keyboard before he had any idea of what he should do. He just tried to look busy.

He had declined to construct a VoiceCommand in his terminal, since he felt it a barrier between him and the labyrinth of the central computer. The computer was comprised of the top seven planner robots, or Supervisors, in the city, joined by their communication links. The central core could only be accessed in the mysterious office inside the Compass Tower, but he had had no use for it since instructing it to discontinue the excessive building and shapechanging of the city. Using only his keyboard to access the computer allowed him to bring up more raw data and to streamline the whole system when he had the time. Now it also allowed him to tinker silently.

After a moment of concentrating, his discomfort was gone. When he spoke, his voice was casual. "Actually, this computer really is kind of stupid. Not the individual Supervisors, of course, but the way they combine their information. The shapechanging loaded so much data into them so fast that they recorded it without organizing it. The computer has become too complex to work well. It needs a lot more streamlining to become efficient."

"I thought you were streamlining it."

"When I get the chance," he snapped, suddenly annoyed again. He was fairly sure he could make some real progress, given time, but he was tired of her always questioning his ability with computers. It was the one subject he actually knew something about, and he had demonstrated it many times over. Since his amnesia had left him with little knowledge of himself, the knowledge he did have was very important to him. He had even learned the kind of amnesia he had, something called "fractionated, retrograde, hypnosis-resistant psychogenic amnesia"—whatever that meant.

Katherine didn't say anything, though he remained aware that she was watching him.

"Well, we *are* stuck with a rather odd computer, after all," he said. Her composure made him self-conscious about his own discomfort. He made an effort to cool off a little. "Here we are in Robot City, a place built and run and populated exclusively by robots, and we have no idea of who created it, or why. I mean, who ever heard of a planet like this?"

"I know," she said gently. "Derec, we are in this together."

"Let me explain the computer again. We're sure the robots have the Key, because there is no one else here on the planet except us. No—"

"Derec, I know this part," she said with exaggerated weariness.

"Let me go on. I'm trying to build up to my point. Look, I've never encountered a computer quite like this, and I'm still trying to think through how to handle it."

"Go on."

"The computer obviously is subject to the Three Laws of Robotics, and that should make it honor my requests for information, under the Second Law. It did not, probably for two reasons. One is prior programming, where the Second Law required the robots collectively to keep certain secrets under orders they received from another human, presumably the creator of Robot City, whoever it was."

The Second Law of Robotics is: "A robot must obey the orders given it by human beings except where such orders would conflict with the First Law."

Katherine nodded quietly, now gazing at the floor. "What's the second reason?"

"The second reason is that the computer system has apparently expanded to the point where it needs fundamental reorganization to operate efficiently. Too many parts of the system just don't seem to know what the other parts know. All sorts of information is lost in there. Even when it does know the answer to a question, sometimes the information takes much too long to locate. And I have to think up special ways of giving orders and asking questions to get it out.

Katherine lifted her head and smiled. "We're both getting better at that, Derec. We've had some practice now, especially with individual robots."

Derec grinned. "I guess I can't argue with that. So far, the best way to make the robots cooperate is to convince them that we're in danger, thus activating their First Law programming."

"I know, I know—have you forgotten my charade on Rockliffe Station with that little alien friend of yours, Wolruf? The trouble is, it's even harder to convince them when we're just debating. I seem to recall that we've both gone a few rounds with various robots that way."

"That's true, too." The positronic brains of the humanoid robots were quite sophisticated, and debating with their cold logic could be frustrating. "The Supervisors were so cooperative—within their limits of programming, of course—that it's too bad we can't just try to work with them to get the Key back."

"They haven't even admitted that they took it from our hiding place on the Compass Tower," said Katherine. "Why would they cooperate with us?"

"I'm sure they wouldn't, or couldn't. That's why we'll have to try locating the Key without confronting them. The longer it takes them to realize that we're after it, the more freedom we'll have."

Despite their current rapport, Derec was afraid that if he didn't stay on the computer, Katherine would make more comments about his incompetence. She might even call him a quitter. Determined not to give her any excuse for that, he continued to play idly on the keyboard.

Katherine pulled up the other chair—they only had two—and sat down. "Derec, let's try to think up some questions I could ask some of the other robots, not the Supervisors. I know they won't answer our direct questions about the Key, but I've gotten information out of them before. Like you were saying, we just have to think up the right questions. Stuff they have to answer because of the Laws."

He nodded. "Or else questions they don't realize will lead us anywhere. The problem is, that's what I've been trying to do through the computer. I guess I just don't know."

All they really knew about the Key to Perihelion was that it was a teleportation device and that it had been taken from the place where they had hidden it. Obviously, the robots had taken it, and so far they had not even revealed that much information. Since the Key seemed to belong here, or at least had some special relationship to Robot City, the robots apparently did not feel that they had stolen it. They were incapable of dishonesty as such.

"We know the robots were searching for the Key for a long time," said Derec. "So whatever they've done with it must have been part of their long-term programming."

He could certainly use her help, but he didn't know if he trusted her enough to speak freely. At one point, he had offered to let her use it to leave the planet while he stayed, and she had chosen to remain here with him. That had been some time ago, though. Sometimes they seemed very close, but he still wasn't sure that if she got to the Key first, she would share its use with him. She had some kind of chronic physical condition—precisely what kind of condition was her secret—and she just might be in a bigger hurry to get off the planet than she claimed.

For that matter, he was worried about her. He wanted to get her some human medical care, and that meant getting away from Robot City. However, he did not want to be left behind.

"What they're *doing* is obvious," said Katherine. "They plan to teleport somewhere. That's all the Key is good for, as far as we know."

"But where do they have to go? The planet is all theirs already, except for us."

"Oh, Derec." She sounded exasperated. "At some point, they're going to teleport off the planet entirely, just like we want to do."

"But why—" Derec stopped. They couldn't possibly know why, because they didn't know the robots' purpose here on the planet in the first place. Discussing the robots' motives would not get them very far. "Well, let's think out loud for a minute. On the asteroid where they found the Key, they were programmed to self-destruct when they were under attack. The Key and the element of secrecy were much more important than the robots or other materials to the person who programmed them. Cost was absolutely not a real concern. And that programming was critically important, since it violated the Third Law."

The Third Law of Robotics is: "A robot must protect his own existence as long as such protection does not conflict with the First or Second Laws."

"So their self-destruction—probably for the purpose of secrecy—must have been programmed by their creator under the First or Second Laws." She thought a moment. "There's that minimalist engineering again, which you keep talking about."

"Now, wait a minute." He turned in his chair to face her. "Haven't I already explained this? When I use that term, I mean these designs that we keep seeing that make things easy to use, even though the technology may have to be much more complicated than necessary to make it that easy." He laughed, glad to have the advantage on her for a change. "What's that got to do with robots melting themselves down into hot puddles of molten junk?"

"Well, it's the same attitude. It's not the engineering as such, but the priorities. The creator of Robot City doesn't care about conserving materials."

"Oh. Well . . . you might have a point, I suppose. Of course, they have all the materials they want, since there is no competition here. I . . . say!" He suddenly turned back to the console. Without mentioning the Key at all, he called up the records of supply requisitions. Then he searched out unusual movements of materials with a top-level priority. Several locations were given. "Ha! What do you bet they've just set up some kind of place to keep the Key?"

"Yes!" Katherine threw her arms around his neck and gave him a quick squeeze. "They must have. Considering how important it is, they'll want it under the tightest security you ever saw on this planet." She laughed. "And if we get too close, maybe these suicidal robots will start melting themselves down into hot little puddles of molten junk again."

Derec had stiffened in surprise at her embrace and felt his face grow hot with embarrassment again. They had been affectionate at times before, but arguments always seemed to follow. He had no idea how she really felt.

Katherine went on excitedly. "Do you suppose a particular robot is in charge? That would tell us who to look for."

Glad to have something else to do, Derec called up a list of duty changes among the robots. That list included geographical changes of assignment where they were pertinent. Major changes in reorganization were still taking place in the wake of the building frenzy that Derec had recently stopped. Now he correlated that information with the list of locations for which an abundance of materiel had just been requisitioned. All at once, he had the number of a single robot. "There it is!"

Katherine was looking over his shoulder. "And, look — it has a huge crew that's just been assigned to work under it. Wow, this serial number is a mouthful." Normally, robots with a lot of human contact were given language names instead of numbers or duty designations, but on Robot City the robots had no reason to assume that human contact would be made with any frequency; only the Supervisors had been given names.

"Watch this. Let's see. Key. . . . How about Keymo?" He hit a sequence of keys.

"What did you do?"

"I've given it a name. It'll be easier for us to remember. Now that it's in the computer, it'll respond to that as well as its number. The other robots can learn it if they ask."

"I didn't know you could do that."

He grinned up at her. "I just figured it out today."

"Congratulations. Say, Derec. . . ."

"Yeah?"

"*Look* at the size of that crew it has assembled. What could they possibly be doing?"

Derec shrugged. "Security? You're right about that part. The robots will have that Key guarded heavily."

"What would they be afraid of on Robot City?" Besides, they can have other kinds of security systems. They don't need a bunch of robots just standing around."

"You got me, kiddo."

"What about their last duties? What kind of skills have they specialized in?"

He started calling up a list of their previous duties, and spoke as he worked. "I know that skills matter to some of the robots, but I'm not sure how much. Certainly, for information, they can all draw upon the central computer. If they can manage to get the data out of that tangled contraption, any one of them can know practically anything that any robot here knows." He looked at the list that came up. "There we are. Hmm—let me try this." In a couple of strokes, he had the computer subdivide the list according to previous duties that the various robots had in common.

"I don't see much of a pattern," Katherine admitted after a moment.

Derec shook his head. "I don't, either. They have all kinds of different backgrounds."

"Maybe they have something else in common. Can you ask the computer to tell you if they have some other common trait?"

"I can ask it anything we can think of." Derec smiled ruefully. "Whether or not I get a civilized answer is another matter." A moment later, he had a new list in front of them. He looked it over and let out a slow breath. "Wow."

"It must be the Key," Katherine said softly.

According to the computer, the robots on this new duty roster had been selected for their absolute peak efficiency. They had recorded the fewest breakdowns, the shortest repair times, and the finest work records. Those who had experienced contact with humans had consistently reached any necessary decisions regarding the Laws with the least time and effort, though of course all the robots reached the correct decisions eventually. This team represented the best robots from all over Robot City.

"This Keymo must be the best of the best," said Derec, "considering that they put him in charge. Tangling with this bunch is going to be tough."

"Think of it this way: if we can talk him out of the Key to Perihelion, we can talk these robots into anything."

Derec looked up at her, smiling weakly. When he caught her eye, they both laughed.

"All right," Katherine conceded. "If we can talk them out of the Key to Perihelion, we won't need anything else from them."

"We should go to Keymo prepared with an argument." Derec got up and walked over to the kitchen area. "And since we can't count on finding food outside our apartment here, we'd better eat first." He looked over the limited list of fare that the chemical processor could simulate. "I'm afraid we're out of the fresh produce. We'll have to request another delivery. Right now, we can't afford the time."

Katherine joined him, peering over his shoulder with a look of distaste. "That's another good reason for us to get off this planet. This stuff tastes terrible."

"The robots did what they could, I guess. Before we got here, they just had no reason to concern themselves with cooking. Maybe we're lucky they could make a chemical processor that's even this tolerable."

"As far as I'm concerned, the best meal out of this machine is the fastest one I can eat, so I don't have to taste it any longer than necessary."

"Fine. We don't want to waste time, anyway." Derec entered the code and turned it on. "Nutrition bars it is—again."

"I'll take the fruit punch to drink, though."

"Yeah—me, too."

A moment later, they each sat down with a dark brown,

warm, rectangular shape. Each bar had a combination of proteins, carbohydrates, and cellulose that would fill them up. The taste was more bland than bad. The chemical processor could also produce more complex meals, which were equally or more nutritious but also equally bland to the taste. It was no match even for the autogalleys on ships.

Derec washed down a mouthful of food with simulated fruit punch. At least the citric acid gave it a strong tang. "If I get the time, I can try ordering the computer to give me some improvements to try on the processor. The trouble is, I don't know what chemicals have to be added to make it taste better . . . and I doubt that the central computer knows, either. Robots have sensory capabilities for analytical purposes, but they don't care about human gourmet preferences."

"If we can get the Key today, we'll be gone, anyway. Let's work on that premise. How are we going to talk Keymo out of the Key?"

"When you put it that way, it sounds a little preposterous, I must admit. Well . . . do you have any ideas?" He was hoping to divert her from his own lack of plans.

"Our only chance is to force him to surrender the Key under some interpretation of the Laws. So we'll have to pose an argument to him, like. . . ." She shrugged, unable to suggest anything.

"If the food were any worse, we could tell him we have to get off the planet or suffer harm." Derec laughed.

"The trouble is, it's not *that* bad."

"We can probably figure that the Second Law by itself won't help us. Like I said about getting information from the central computer, any request from us will almost certainly be overridden by prior programming orders under the Second Law. Whoever created Robot City got his instructions in first."

Katherine looked down at her glass, and picked it up even though it was empty. Suddenly she got up and went to the processor to fill it. Then she just stood there looking at the glass.

Derec had no idea why her manner had just turned chilly. He reflected that it figured, somehow; just as he became comfortable enough to joke around a little, she started to withdraw from him again. He watched her without speaking.

Katherine turned and walked into her room.

Derec, feeling snubbed, did not try to approach her. Instead, he got up and carried their plates and glasses to the washer. After turning it on, he straightened up a little and wiped the inside of the chemical processor's delivery receptacle. He could not tell what she was doing.

Once again, Derec felt trapped by his own circumstances. Some time ago, he had awakened in a lifepod from a larger spacecraft with no memory of his name or his earlier life. Even the name "Derec" had been adopted only so that he could call himself something. He had had a number of crazy adventures since that time, but none of them had brought his memory back.

He had met Katherine along the way, and they had formed a partnership of necessity. After all, even now they were the only humans of the planet, and shared a desire to get off Robot City. He still found her difficult to deal with. Nevertheless, if they were going to get off Robot City, they would have to get the Key to Perihelion. Derec took a deep breath.

"Katherine?"

"Yes." Her voice was low and listless.

"Are you, um, feeling okay?"

"Yes!" She spoke sharply, almost too insistently.

"I suppose we ought to go visit Keymo, wherever he is. You still want to go, don't you?"

"Of course I want to go," she snapped, coming to the doorway. "Why wouldn't I want to go?"

"*I* don't know!" Derec threw up his arms. "Sometimes you're as big a mystery to me as the origin of Robot City."

Katherine pushed past him and turned. "Well?"

"Well what?"

"Are we going now or what? You were in such a big hurry."

"Sure! Sure, we're going. I'm in a big hurry to get off this planet, and I thought you were, too. Come on, let's go!"

"All right!"

Seething with anger, Derec stalked out of their quarters, aware that she was right behind him.

CHAPTER 2
THROUGH THE CHUTE

Outside, the great pyramidal Compass Tower glittered in the sunlight. It was taller by half than any other structure in the city, and stood as a familiar landmark. Below it, the skyline was a varied line of spires, domes, cubes, and towers.

Derec and Katherine rode the slidewalk in silence. He had an idea of where to find Keymo, since the ongoing shapechanging of the city had been discontinued—although the robots still renovated and built constantly. One of the many benefits of ending the shapechanging was that the robots had been building a coherent system of slidewalks for pedestrian traffic. Still, finding one's way around Robot City remained a challenge.

His anger was cooling quickly. In the distance ahead, he could see a large dome on the horizon, a brilliant, shining bronze in color. It was near the site of Keymo's operation, and Derec guessed it was the Key Center itself.

"I noticed a similar dome here once," she said, also gazing at it. "Any idea what it is?"

"Not exactly, no."

"What does that mean?"

He glanced at her warily, thinking he had detected an edge in her voice, but she was still looking up at the building. He raised his gaze again, still walking. "Well, actually . . . what I mean is, sometimes the robots have to house a certain class of facilities that can't be fit into normal industrial bays or doors. I haven't looked closely at any of these domes, but I think they're used for stuff like that."

"I don't see any doors, now that you mention it. I suppose they're on the other side. The Key is small enough to carry, though. I don't see why they would need a gigantic dome for it."

"Maybe that's not the place." Derec shrugged. "Maybe the Key Center is in a mud hut next door."

"Very funny. If that particular dome is new, I'm betting it was set up for the Key."

"I'm not arguing. But we have to get off the slidewalk. It's being fixed up or something just ahead. There isn't a functioning one to take us from here to there."

"I hope you don't expect me to walk that far!" She stepped off the slidewalk with him.

A small function robot, the class without the positronic brains, skittered out of her way. It was a small scrap collector, gathering debris as it moved on a cushion of short, nimble legs around a construction site. It was heading for a sewer chute in which to deposit its load.

A humanoid robot, of the foreman class in the city, approached them. The sunlight shone on the distinctive, helmeted head and blue skin.

"Identify yourself," Katherine ordered.

"I am Construction Foreman 391." The robot's eyes, deep in the darkness of its horizontal eyeslit, focused on her.

"What is the most convenient way for us to reach—Derec, tell it where."

He noted that she had spoken to him in the same imperious tone she used with the robots. "We're going to that dome, or somewhere close to it. It's about 6.4 kilometers."

"Frost!" She turned on him. "You weren't going to walk that far, were you?"

"Of course not."

"Perhaps the vacuum chute would be safe for humans," said Foreman 391. "You must ask a chute foreman. May the maintenance robot resume its duties?"

"Oh—of course." Katherine glanced down at the scrap collector, which she had inadvertently trapped against the sewer chute. It whirred patiently at her feet until she moved out of the way. Then it headed back into the construction site.

"A vacuum chute?" Derec asked. "I don't remember anything about a vacuum chute before. That's pretty archaic technology, too."

"Yes. It is being used because a new facility in Robot City is producing a strong partial vacuum as a side effect. Utilizing this side effect constitutes an efficient use of energy."

"Say, you're rather proud of that, aren't you?" Derec grinned with amusement. "You must have worked on the vacuum chutes, huh?"

"This is not pride. It is recognition that certain principles of efficiency have been successfully executed. Yes, all the construction foremen at my level had to be consulted when the chute system was routed through the city."

"Forget the frosted chutes," Katherine said irritably. "What about that big bronze dome?"

"What about it?"

"Well, you're a construction foreman. You must know what it's for."

"Yes."

"Would you tell us, please?"

Derec hid a smile at her frustration. At times she had handled robots very well, but today did not seem to be her day. In fact, both of them occasionally reached the point where they were infuriated by the literal interpretations that the robots made of human speech.

"These designs are used to house extremely large or oddly shaped facilities of all kinds. The—"

"Excuse me," said Derec. "But would an extremely important facility, one that had special priority, be in one of those domes, also?"

"I have no role in decision-making of that kind."

"But from your experience in Robot City, do you think it might be likely?"

"The materials used in the construction of the dome do not offer any special advantage, based on the premise you have given."

Derec sighed. "Okay. What is this stuff, anyhow?"

"Are you referring to the construction material?"

"Yes." Derec gritted his teeth, and caught Katherine suppressing a smile this time.

"The external shell is the only significant distinction of material these domes possess. It is comprised of a material called dianite. Dianite is a specialized form of the modular material from which all of Robot City is constructed. This substance has a number of unusual qualities. In its solid form it is extremely hard, yet very light in weight and with high tensile strength. However, its most unusual property is that—"

"Okay, okay, thank you. Is there a method of normal transportation that will take us there? From here?"

"Normally, this slidewalk would take you there. While it is under modification, no normal transportation is available that will do this."

"What about those chutes?" Katherine asked.

"Allow me to consult the central computer. Yes, one of them is on a direct line from here to a stop near your destination. You understand that a chute foreman must be consulted for matters of safety?"

"Right," said Derec. "Where do we find one?"

"The nearest chute stop is two blocks forward and one block left. I must resume my duties."

"Come on!" Katherine took off at a run.

They ran along the motionless slidewalk as long as they could, then jumped off and ran along its shoulder. Here and there, they had to skip around functioning robots going about their business, and past a couple of foremen, as well. In moments, they had turned left at the corner and had come skidding up to a small loading dock. A foreman robot was standing on the dock, watching a small function robot use an armlike crane to lift a container.

The function robot was hoisting molded containers from a long, transparent tube that lay horizontally alongside the dock.

"We need that," Katherine said briskly. "How does it work?"

"It is pulled through the chute by a powerful vacuum," said the foreman. "What is your need for it?"

"Identify yourself."

"I am Chute Foreman 34." The robot looked back and forth

between them. "I have never had direct contact with humans before."

Katherine threw her arms up in a gesture of impatience that Derec knew all too well. He was glad not to be the cause of it this time.

"Yes, we're humans. Congratulations, genius. Now—"

Derec rushed to get in front of her, surprised at her sudden aggressiveness. "We're going to that dome. A construction foreman suggested we inquire as to whether a vacuum chute would be safe for us to travel in."

Chute Foreman 34 glanced down at the tube. From here, Derec could see that it was resting in a siding away from the vacuum chute itself.

"Yes, this tube is safe for cargo more fragile than humans. It has ventilation and padding. However, it may not be comfortable."

"How uncomfort—" Derec started.

"Frost that; we'll take it." Katherine pushed Derec aside and climbed down into the open tube.

Derec followed her and found that, while the slick cushion was padded well enough, they had to recline along the length of the transparent tube for the door to slide shut. He found himself lying against her, and moved over self-consciously.

"I will send you to the stop nearest the dome," said the robot, just before it secured the door.

"I hope it has more experience with these chutes than it has with humans," said Katherine.

Derec wiggled a little to get more comfortable, his gaze aimed upward at the sky. He began to speak, but the jolting start of the tube interrupted the effort. With a great rushing of air, it accelerated quickly and shot into a black chute.

Air was swirling within the tube. Apparently, the ventilation consisted of carefully shaped openings in the back of the tube, which pulled some air into the tube as it was drawn along. He was trying to figure out how that could work when suddenly the chute curved upward. All at once, he felt himself sliding head first, on his back, toward the rear of the tube. Laughing, he and Katherine clutched at each other and tried vainly to brace themselves against the smooth sides of the tube.

Light flooded the tube, nearly blinding Derec. When he

could focus his eyes, he and Katherine both shouted and grabbed at each other again. The chute was now as transparent as the tube, and they were shooting along high above the ground. Just ahead, the chute wound between two large buildings. Though Derec knew better, he felt his whole body tighten reflexively with the fear that they were about to smash into one of the walls.

Katherine apparently felt the same, inhaling sharply just as they plunged into the gap between the buildings. The sides of the buildings were a blur all around them. The chute then swerved upward again, keeping them both pinned against the rear of the tube, braced with their arms held above their heads.

The buildings first fell away on her side, then on his. He felt his stomach seem to drop as he watched rooftops recede below him. Traveling in enclosed spacecraft was one thing, but actually watching the ground fall from him triggered all the instinctive fears of height that his ancient ancestors had acquired by falling out of trees. Beside him, Katherine was giggling nervously.

The chute leveled off, and Derec let out a cautious breath.

She turned to face him, just inches away. "Pretty wild, huh?"

He grinned, but didn't trust himself to speak.

Now that they were speeding along a level section of the chute, he was able to relax a little. When he took a tentative look off to the side, he found that most of the city was now below them, but a few of the tallest towers and obelisks could still throw a shadow over the chute at the right hour. He guessed that the erratic route of the chute was due to the recent discontinuation of the automatic shapechanging in the city. New developments were more likely to be built around existing structures now.

The city was strikingly pretty from this height, and it stretched as far as he could see from his cramped position. Suddenly, the tube plunged steeply downward, and Derec gasped as he found himself staring almost straight down at a drop of several hundred meters. He felt himself sliding toward the front of the tube and clawed futilely for a handhold.

Katherine was also flailing about, and they wound up throwing their arms around each other. The speed of the tube was such, however, that they did not actually fall to the front of the tube. It was accelerating, and Derec felt his ears pop from the sudden change in altitude. He hadn't even noticed the pressure change on their startling ascent.

Finally, the tube leveled off again, smoothly, and then gently rose again just enough to decelerate and come to an easy stop. Derec lay where he was for a moment, looking at Katherine. She smiled and looked away as they untangled themselves.

The tube door opened and another foreman looked down at them. "Unusual cargo," the robot said. "You are unharmed?"

Derec and Katherine laughed as they climbed out, nodding in reassurance. He noticed that she had lost her hard edge somewhere on the breathtaking ride.

"There it is," said Katherine.

The dome rose up right in front of them, the great bronze surface nearly blinding them in the bright sunlight. The dianite had a very fine, pebbled texture, which saved them from an even worse glare. High above them, the curve of the dome carried the top out of sight.

"I don't see a door anywhere," said Derec.

They started walking around the base of the dome, looking all over its nearly smooth, unbroken surface. It was even higher than Derec had guessed from a distance. It had no visible seams or openings of any kind.

When the tunnel stop came into view again, they knew they had walked all the way around the base of the dome. Derec stopped, still looking up for any hint of how to enter. He supposed an opening was possible at the top, but placing it there seemed out of character for Robot City.

Katherine brushed her fingertips along the dianite. "It's pretty."

"Yeah." Derec rapped on the hard surface experimentally. "I suppose we could stand out here and shout, but I doubt anyone inside would hear us."

Katherine faced the dome and backed away, searching the even curve again.

He had taken just a few steps to follow her when he heard a muted ripping sound behind him. When he looked back, he saw the dianite opening in a jagged line where they had been standing, as though invisible hands were tearing it. As they watched, the blue-skinned form of a humanoid robot stepped out.

Katherine drew herself up. "Take us to Keymo," she ordered firmly.

"This is a security area. What is your business with Keymo?" The robot asked.

"Identify yourself," she demanded.

"I am Security 1K. What is your business with Keymo?"

"He must give us the Key to Perihelion."

Derec stepped beside her, afraid that her direct, rather arrogant approach was going to backfire if they didn't offer some kind of explanation. "According to the Second Law, you must obey our orders. After you take us to Keymo, we will instruct him to hand over the Key. Let's go." He started forward confidently, though it was only a bluff.

Security 1K did not take the bluff. It did not move aside at all. "No."

Derec stepped back, not wanting to challenge the robot's physical prowess. He knew that the positronic brains in the robots were reliable, so his earlier assumption seemed to be true: the robots were operating under Second Law instructions, certainly from the mysterious holder of the office in the Compass Tower. That suggested a new argument to him.

"Hold it," said Derec. "Look. Apparently you have a very strong Second Law imperative that you are operating on, established previously. Okay. But that was a general instruction, I'll bet. Right?"

"That is right. The need for security in this matter is part of the entire project of this facility."

"But I'm giving you a specific and important order right now. I believe that should override a general instruction relying on broadly based programming." Actually, he wasn't sure he believed that at all, but it was worth a try.

Security 1K hesitated. When the positronic brain of a robot paused long enough for a human to notice, the argument had at least been considered worth an internal debate.

"No," the robot said, after what was for it a considerable length of time. "The earlier imperative stands."

Derec sighed, but he wasn't surprised.

"Our well-being is at stake," Katherine declared. "We must consult with Keymo. Your prevention of this violates the First Law."

"How?" Security 1K asked.

"We can't thrive in a city full of robots. We need other people around us."

As the robot continued to debate with Katherine, Derec looked at the open edge of the dianite. It seemed oddly familiar, especially in its texture, but he couldn't figure out why. The substance offered no sign of any frame. It looked quite thin, and seemed to constitute the entire wall.

"You are in no danger," Security 1K was saying. "This is not a First Law problem."

She glanced at Derec, who shrugged. The robot was backing into the dome again. A moment later, the two sides of the dianite seemed to straighten and grow together.

Carefully, Derec tapped the former opening, afraid it might be hot. It was not, so he ran his hand over the wall in that area. The surface seemed fully integral with the rest of the wall. He looked at Katherine and raised his eyebrows.

"Katherine, whoever's behind the creation of this city is some kind of genius. Maybe the robots invented this dianite and maybe they didn't, but somebody created them. This stuff would be worth a fortune off this planet, just like so many other things here."

She spun away and started walking quickly along the base of the dome.

Astonished, he watched her for a moment, then went into sputtering rage. "What is *wrong* with you? You've been acting crazy all day—come back here!" He ran after her.

Katherine had stiffened at his shouts, and had then begun walking faster. At the sound of his running footsteps, she broke into a run, also. He slowed to a walk, realizing that if she was truly determined not to talk, catching her wouldn't help any.

Then he whirled angrily and slammed his fist against the wall. "Hey! Open up in there!" He pounded on the dianite a few more times. Then he stepped back, breathing hard.

A new hole tore open in the wall and Security 1K appeared in the opening. It did not step out this time. "Do you have further business here?"

"Yes! Bring Keymo out here!" It felt good to yell at somebody, and the robot couldn't just walk away.

"If you do not have new reasons to see him, I request that

you stop instructing me to listen to you. Do you have new reasons?"

"Uh—" Derec glanced down the way for Katherine, who had stopped to watch. "Well. . . ."

"Please avoid unnecessary contact with this facility," said Security 1K. It backed away from the opening, which began to heal again.

Derec watched in frustration as the substance quickly closed. On an impulse, he leaned against a solid portion of the wall and pulled off one of his boots. He stuck it into the small portion of the hole that still remained and kept a careful eye on the dianite as it grew together. Now he remembered why it was familiar— the substance was similar to the material out of which these robots were made, possibly even a cellular material. He had had experience with these robot parts when he had created the robot Alpha. That had occurred long before he had reached Robot City, but after his amnesia had come on him. This dianite did not seem to be alive, exactly, but it certainly had some startling properties.

The dianite grew around the boot—and stopped, much to his relief. He had been afraid it would simply keep growing together even if it had to cut right through the boot. Instead, his boot had been incorporated into the wall as part of it.

He leaned down close and prodded the dianite around his boot with his fingers. He was right—the tearing sound had given away the secret. This stuff was very hard as an integral unit, but once the tear was started it was quite fragile, and even grew limp within a short radius of the tear. He was able to pull a few of the modular cells apart with his fingers now. The tear could be opened again.

He just hoped no one on the other side was in a position to see him.

"Katherine! Come on!" He gently began tearing the wall upward like fabric. It was tough, but it gave. When he looked up, she hadn't moved. "Come on—" He lowered his voice, suddenly aware that he had a sizable opening in the wall, nearly enough to crawl through . . . or be heard through.

Katherine turned and started walking away.

Derec wanted to shout, but didn't dare. Then, clenching his jaw, he crawled into the opening, leaving his boot behind to hold the breach as the wall grew together again behind him. He would have a talk with her later.

He found himself on the floor behind a large, bulky piece of machinery. The sounds of robots moving about reached him, but most would be function robots. He did not hear any voices. Of course, the foremen had their comlinks for communication with each other.

He spotted Security 1K sitting high on a stool at the far side of the dome, monitoring a console that probably reported a number of effects that would include the vibrations in the wall that Derec and Katherine had caused by touching and punching it. Since 1K was still at the console, Derec judged that the monitor had accepted the boot as part of the wall. Certainly, the wall had grown in solidly around it.

A ceiling was just over the security console, signifying at least one upper floor, if not more. The interior curve of the dome was out of sight above it. On the floor, the entire crew of robots assigned to Keymo seemed to be working on different pieces of equipment that varied greatly in size. One foreman was seated at a computer console on the floor beneath the raised seat of Security 1K. Derec guessed that this was Keymo, and started working his way through the machines to reach the robot without being noticed.

Derec knew that he would not have much time. Even as he crawled over cables on the floor and between different machine housings, he wondered if he should just stand up, run over to Keymo and start talking right away. As it was, Security 1K might become alerted to his presence and throw him out before he could start his pitch.

He stopped to get his bearings. Keymo was much closer now, studying the readings on the console. It looked like a good time to approach the robot.

Security 1K had not moved.

If Katherine had come in with him, one of them could have provided a diversion while the other spoke to Keymo. But it was too late for that now. He took another deep breath and stood up.

He felt totally exposed and vulnerable as he walked across the floor, but his presence caused no noticeable stir among the robots. When he reached Keymo's desk, the chief robot of the facility looked up.

"I require the Key to Perihelion," Derec said formally. He edged to the side of the console and peeked at the readouts.

"You would be the human Derec," said Keymo. "Giving you the Key is not possible."

"We must get off the planet in order to survive. The Key is our only means of transportation."

"What is the danger to you and your companion on this planet?"

"Well, we just aren't supposed to live on a planet of robots. We need the company of other humans. Uh. . . ." He knew this line of debate was weak, but it was all he had. The exact nature of Katherine's chronic condition was unknown to him, and therefore too vague to use.

"That is not a danger by itself."

"That's what I told him," said a voice behind Derec.

He tried to turn, but felt firm hands under his arms that lifted him off his feet. It was Security 1K, of course, and Derec did not bother to protest as he was carted to the wall like a lump of waste matter. He could not see how the robot opened a new slit in the wall, but he noted that the boot was elsewhere, and apparently still unnoticed. It would provide another opportunity later.

He was deposited gently but unceremoniously outside the wall, where he stood awkwardly on one booted foot. Behind him, the wall grew together. Katherine walked slowly toward him and stopped.

"I could have used you in there," he growled.

"I didn't realize you'd get in. Then I didn't know what to do." She stared at the ground in front of her.

"Let's get out of here."

Derec was in no mood for another crazy ride in the vacuum chute, and he didn't want to talk to her until they were in private. He hitched rides for them on the top of an enclosed transport vehicle, and on the exterior ladders of a vehicle the purpose of which Derec could not divine. As long as the robot drivers judged their human passengers to be riding safely, they had no objection. Katherine was withdrawn all the way home, and he left her alone.

When they had returned, he went right back to the console. She reluctantly stood behind him with her arms folded. He kept his mind on his work with an effort.

"Did you learn anything while you were inside?" she asked quietly.

"A little," he said coldly. "It might amount to something and it might not. I read an entry number on Keymo's console, and I'm running it through the central computer."

"Are you sure it's really the Key Center?"

"Don't you remember? We demanded to see Keymo, and the security robot didn't deny he was in there. I demanded the Key from the top robot, and he didn't deny having it."

"Okay, okay."

He paused to study the information that had come up. She came closer to read over his shoulder.

"It's a list of substances, mostly metals and synthetics. Percentages of each one . . . energy consumption in the dome."

"Look on the right," said Katherine. "That's the designation for hyperspace. It's an experiment of some kind, consuming air."

"Air—the chutes! The vacuum chutes. That's why they're using such an old technology. What did that construction robot say? The vacuum is a side effect of something else going on. This is it."

"But what is it?" She asked cautiously.

He started an angry retort, then decided to have it out with her after he had finished considering this information. In the long run, it was more important. "I'm taking another look at that supply requisition we saw earlier. All the same substances are listed, in the same percentages. I wonder. . . ."

"They're duplicating the Key."

"You think so?"

"I'm sure of it, Derec. And, look at the addendum on the supply requisition. They added small amounts there at the dome."

"That would be the original Key," Derec said slowly. "They . . . had to break it down to analyze it. Then they tossed the pieces into the pool of materials. It's gone."

"But they're making more. Derec, this will make it easier for us to get one. Instead of one Key under careful guard, they'll have a bunch of them we can try for."

"I just hope Keymo is duplicating them accurately. And we might have to wait for them to turn out a few. We can't get something that hasn't been made yet."

"Uh, Derec? Would you turn around?"

He turned in his chair and looked up at her.

"I guess you deserve an explanation. I know I've been acting weird. And I'm sorry I didn't go inside with you. I had my mind on something else at the wrong time."

"The wrong time!" Derec leaped out of his chair, glad to have the opening. "The worst possible time! We might have gotten the Key—or *a* key, anyway!"

"Derec, please. I'm trying to explain. Anyway, maybe there weren't any to get, like you said."

"All right! All right. Go ahead and explain." He paced away from her and turned at the wall. "Go ahead."

"Derec, I know who designed Robot City. And why."

"What?"

"I—"

"Why didn't you tell me?" He raged. "No! Never mind that —who did build this place?" His astonishment and curiosity were interfering with his anger.

"Before I get to that, my real name is Ariel Welsh."

"Well—glad to meet you. Finally."

"I'm the only daughter of Juliana Welsh, of the planet Aurora." She watched for his reaction.

"Should that mean something to me?"

"I thought you might have heard of her—she's extremely wealthy. Lots of people have."

Derec shrugged.

"My mother was the biggest patron of a man called Dr. Avery. Have you heard of him?"

"Dr. Avery. You know, I think I have . . . his name sounds familiar. What about him?"

"Dr. Avery was the brain behind all this." She waved a hand, indicating the entire planet. "Robot City is his. And my mother's money got it started."

Derec's heart began to pound. Dr. Avery. He had sat in the man's office and used his terminal; now he had a name to go with the vague, limited information. Someone had been in that office shortly before he had; he had found a recently discarded food container.

"Whew. You really were keeping a secret, weren't you?" He spoke more sympathetically. "What was he doing? Why did he build it?"

"From what Mom said, I think he was a famous architect.

She called him a visionary. He was also eccentric, and used to argue with everyone. Robot City was a place where he could test his theories."

"I get it. Here's this . . . genius, I suppose, with all these outlandish ideas that no one can handle. So he wants to try out his experiments without interference, and your mother finances him."

Katherine—now Ariel—nodded. "She gave him enough to get started, with the understanding that his project would have to be self-supporting after a certain point. Since that was part of his experiment, he didn't object. And of course the robots are always very efficient."

"He wanted to create an ongoing, self-sufficient city?"

"With a fully functioning society."

"Where is he now?"

"He vanished a long time ago. Just went off somewhere. I suppose he's dead, but Mom said he's so strange that you just never know."

"And he left behind an entire city of robots running on their original programming." Derec shook his head. "Well, that clears up more than you think."

"Like what?"

"When the microbes from the blood of . . . of the dead man set off the automatic shapechanging in the city, this entire community went berserk because its programming made an interpretation that no human would have made."

"In other words," said Ariel, "something went wrong and Dr. Avery wasn't around to fix it. He wanted an ideal experimental environment and he didn't quite get it."

"When you put it that way, though, he came pretty close. If he had stayed here, he might have kept it going the way he wanted."

"There's something else." She looked at her hands, and started playing with her fingernails. "I've been banished from Aurora. I can't go back."

"*You've* been banished? How? I mean, what for? Did you break a law or something? Are you a criminal?"

She gave a wry sneer. "I wish. I'd be a lot better off. Derec, I'm—sick."

"The chronic condition you've mentioned." He spoke gently,

allowing her whatever leeway she wished in such a personal matter.

"Oh, don't worry. You're in no danger. You can't get it from just being around me." She laughed bitterly. "I had an affair. I guess it was, you know, a rebellion against my mother and all her fancy friends. They all expected me to be such a good little girl and grow up to be just like them." It was her turn to start pacing.

Derec waited patiently.

"The guy was a Spacer from, I don't know, some other planet. He was just traveling through, you might say, and he was long gone by the time I found out he'd contaminated me."

"Couldn't your mother help? With all her money and everything?"

"Ha! They don't have any cure on Aurora—or maybe anywhere. Besides, this wasn't just a matter of getting sick and getting well. On Aurora, this is a deadly sin. My mother bought a ship and outfitted it for me, complete with a couple of robots as aides. Getting away was the best I could do."

"Your mother made quite a contribution, at that. You left Aurora in style, at least."

"I can't complain about that."

"And after you left?"

"I told myself I was looking for a cure, but I don't know if I really believe there is such a thing. But I *did* decide not to waste any time!"

Derec felt a prickling along the back of his neck. "What do you mean, not waste any time?"

"Derec, I . . . I'm going to die of this!" And suddenly she was crying, scared and vulnerable in a way he had never seen before.

He hesitated just a moment, and then went to her, holding her—awkwardly at first, then gently as she relaxed against him and really began to sob.

He was dumbfounded. This flood of information seemed to short-circuit his attention, and left him simply staring at the floor without thoughts as she cried in his arms. He had to sort out what he could—that she was Ariel, not Katherine, and that she was not, right now, the confident and sharp-edged older girl he had known her to be.

She was Ariel Welsh, banished from her home planet, trapped on Robot City, and infected with a deadly disease.

He turned her gently by the shoulders and led her into her room. First he sat with her on the bed, still uncertain of what to do. Then, after her sobs had grown fainter, she squeezed his arm affectionately and pulled away to stretch out on the bed. He rose, patted her on the shoulder shyly, and went out, closing her door behind him.

Derec sat at his computer console for a long time without turning it on. His own amnesia suddenly seemed like a fairly manageable problem. Yet the urgency of getting her off Robot City, and perhaps to some medical help, was greater than ever.

He doubted that the robots could help with a disease, at least in the short term. Even so, he started calling up various medical subjects on the central computer, in case Dr. Avery had left anything useful.

Actually, he found quite a bit of medical information pertaining to humans, but nothing that hinted at an ability to find cures for new diseases. The computer did have a list of vaccines, cures, and treatments for diseases he recognized—common ones that would have been available on Aurora. He also found a great deal of advanced material on surgery, organ regeneration, and other treatments for injuries. Overall, however, the library was oddly lacking, as though Dr. Avery, or at least somebody, had just grabbed information and entered it without checking it. For instance, there was no introductory reference on anatomy as such, or on psychology. Derec suspected that the eccentric Dr. Avery had been so involved with the frontiers of science that he had neglected to supply fundamental knowledge. After all, the robots had no particular need for this subject. He also remembered that the library on the planetoid where he had first met these Avery robots had been oddly selected.

At dinner time, he took a break and knocked lightly on Ariel's door. When she did not answer, he peeked inside and found her sleeping soundly. He made dinner for himself and returned to the computer.

The only information he could find pertaining to human anatomy regarded external appearance. This came from the positronic brains of the robots, rather than any specific entry into the computer. They could only obey the Three Laws of Robotics if they could identify humans when they came into contact with them, so he was not surprised to find this. When he saw the addendum beneath it, however, he sat up straight in his chair.

The computer noted five alien presences in Robot City. He supposed that meant humans, as the likelihood of sentient non-human aliens was very slim. There simply weren't enough of them, and he decided that the central computer would surely have made more of the matter. Nor would it ever again interpret microscopic human parasites as alien presences. Non-Avery robots could conceivably be here, of course, but he was sure that the significance of reporting these presences was to warn the local robot population that humans were here. Their presence would bring the Laws into consideration, while the arrival of other robots would not.

Obviously, he and Ariel were two of the five presences, but that left three of whom he had no knowledge. One of the three had arrived just a few days before. The other two, apparently traveling together, had been here for a slightly longer period.

The only ways they could have gotten here were with another Key to Perihelion, if there was another one off the planet, or in spacecraft. Either way, they offered additional chances for Derec and Ariel to get away from Robot City. He stayed on the computer all evening, trying to find more information.

He also rigged the chemical processor to make a new boot. It didn't match, being made of organic materials instead of synthetics, but it fit well enough.

He finally quit for the night when he felt his concentration slipping. After getting something else to eat from the chemical processor, he fell into bed. Ariel was still asleep.

Derec was exhausted, but as he lay in the dark, his mind was still racing. He kept reviewing his new knowledge over and over—Ariel Welsh, her disease, the duplication of the Key . . . and now, three more humans on Robot City—which might mean, possibly, some new ways to get off the planet. Finally, just before he drifted off to sleep, he heard Ariel leave her room and turn on the chemical processor. For tonight, at least, she was all right.

When Derec emerged for breakfast the next morning, clean and dressed, Ariel was working at the computer. He was hesi-

tant to interrupt her there. However, she looked up when he
turned on the chemical processor.

"Morning, Derec." She smiled shyly. "Are you still mad at
me?"

"No. I guess you had good reason to be upset."

"I just felt so guilty and confused about everything. Especially keeping secrets from you, when you were wondering
about the city and all. I'm really sorry."

"I'm just glad you finally told me. In the long run, maybe my
knowing that stuff will help us."

"I saw the file you left on the console, the medical one. You
were trying to help me, weren't you?"

"Yeah. I'm afraid there wasn't much about diseases, though.
But did you see that we're not alone?" He took his breakfast out
of the processor and sat down next to her, his plate on his lap.

"Yes! I was just looking at the notation. Do you have any
idea who they could be?"

"No, I don't. As soon as I've finished eating, I'll see if I can
find any more information about them in the computer, but I'm
not too optimistic. Until I get more streamlining done, this
computer can know all kinds of things and not realize it, you
might say."

"This is such a strange place." Ariel sighed. "When I left
Aurora, I was looking for adventure as well as a cure. I got the
adventure part, such as it is."

"Like getting captured by that pirate, Aranimas?" Derec
grinned. "When he got hold of me, I wasn't looking for adventure at all."

"We made a pretty good team, though, taking care of ourselves in that situation."

"Don't forget the rest of the team—Alpha, the robot I put
together out of all those parts, and Wolruf."

"That little alien. I wonder what happened to them."

"Yeah." He was quiet for a moment, thinking about them.
When he and Ariel had used the Key, and as a result had arrived
in Robot City, Alpha and Wolruf had been left behind.

"Wolruf could be so surprising. One minute, she seemed like
a very shy, subservient little creature, and the next minute we
were relying on her for our lives."

"That's true. And Alpha's certainly unique, since I had to

cobble him together out of random parts. Did I tell you he has a special arm? It's made of a kind of cellular substance. I ordered him to move it as though it's jointed like everyone else's, but actually he can make it completely flexible, like a tentacle. I wonder where they are now."

"We've never really talked about this, before, have we? About our being friends, I mean, and what we've done together."

He looked up at her. She was more at ease than he had ever seen her. He, too, felt the difference. Somehow, he trusted her now, though for all he knew, she could be keeping other secrets. She didn't act like she was.

"Derec, you've been very understanding. I appreciate it. Thank you."

"Uh. . . ." He gave just a hint of a shrug. "That's okay. Now, let's see if we can figure out how to get off the planet."

Derec and Ariel took turns on the console all morning. This gave him a break every so often and gave her some practice. He sat looking over her shoulder as they tried to think up more questions to ask the computer.

"Derec, do you think the strangers that we're looking for have been able to hide? Or disguise themselves?"

"Maybe, but I don't see how. If they tried to hide, they'd still find robots everywhere in Robot City. They would have to stay inside someplace, and even then, they might be in a building that was scheduled for modification or tearing down by the robots." He laughed. "That would give them a good shock."

"And disguising themselves as robots might be a little difficult." She turned, also laughing, to catch his eye.

"Or maybe we could get some scrap robot parts ourselves, and wear them around like ancient armor." Derec shook his head, still grinning. "Especially those helmetlike heads."

"Seriously, though. What could have happened to them?"

"Well, it's possible that there are more sightings that have been lost in the central computer someplace. Otherwise, I don't really have an answer."

"I've asked about all the questions I can think of. I don't know what else to do."

"Let's try another train of thought," said Derec. "We don't know who they are—but what are they coming here for? What do they want?"

"The Key!"

"That's my guess. But other space traffic could come this way, even though we seem to be off the beaten track here. How about this: they knew Dr. Avery and came here to take over. Or what about your mother—could she have sent someone here to check on her investment?"

"I don't believe my mother actually knows where Robot City is, or maybe even exactly what it is."

"That narrows it to two possibilities I can think of. Either they're travelers who arrived by chance, maybe for repairs or fuel, or they came for the Key and maybe to take over Robot City. Can you think of anything else?"

"Maybe Avery himself, if he isn't dead. I doubt that, though. He'd be in his office running things, not allowing these chance sightings. But what are we going to do?"

"We'll have to go out and look around for ourselves, I guess. Unless you have another suggestion."

She shook her head.

"We'll have to be careful, though, till we find out who they are and what they want. We've gotten used to a certain amount of security here with the robots, since they can't hurt us, but now that's changed."

"Not as long as we have robots around us. Remember, they can't stand by and allow us to come to harm, either. What about asking Avernus or one of the other Supervisors to help us find them?"

"Not right now. I don't want to alert the Supervisors to our interest in getting the Key, and so far they've left us alone. Let's start by going back to the Key Center. If we can get our hands on a key, we can just leave Robot City to fend for itself."

This time they took standard transportation, even though it took them farther out of their way than the vacuum chute had. The subway tunnels were another development that had become feasible once the shapechanging had stopped. They were full of robots, going about their daily business, who could be questioned. Derec and Ariel went to the nearest tunnel stop and rode down the ramp.

Traffic in the tunnels took the form of a robot, or a human, standing on a meter-square platform, enclosed by a booth of transparent walls, with a small console that could be set for whatever stop the passenger wished. The platforms ran on tracks; some parts of the city had as many as fifteen parallel tracks. The tunnel computer, an offshoot of the central computer, did all the steering, and could shift platforms from one track to another in order to create the most efficient flow of traffic. Tunnel stops had additional siding loops for loading and unloading. The technology reminded Derec of the lift system he had seen on the asteroid where he had first encountered the Avery robots.

Without positronic brains, the function robots could not set the controls, so only humans and robots with positronic brains rode the booths. Derec observed, as he watched the robots speed past, that they all stood motionless and staring straight ahead, unlike humans, who of course would be shifting positions, shuffling their feet, and looking around. The robots were logical, but never curious.

Ahead of them, several robots were emerging from platform booths. Derec and Ariel split up to approach them.

Derec stood directly in front of one to make sure the robot could see him clearly as a human in the dim light. "Just a moment. I would like to ask you a few questions."

"Yes?" The robot stopped.

"Have you seen any humans?"

"I presume you mean other than yourself."

"Yeah, besides me."

"Your companion is a female human."

"Besides us!" Derec flung up his hands. "Somewhere else in the city. Anywhere."

"No. You are the first humans I have ever seen."

"Thanks." Derec sighed and flagged down another robot. "Have you seen any humans other than my companion and myself?"

"What companion?"

"Uh—her. Over there. See her?"

"Yes."

"You have? Where?"

"Over there. Where you pointed."

"What—no, not her—"

"You asked if I saw her. I said yes."

"Okay, okay. Now, then. Other than the two of us present right here, have you ever seen any humans on Robot City?"

"No."

"All right, thanks." Derec waved him on.

At the moment, no more robots were coming into the siding loop or down the ramp. Ariel joined him.

"No luck here," she said. "You get anything?"

"No. Let's ride out to the Key Center."

They got into the first empty booth. It was a fairly close fit, but not uncomfortable. Derec set the controls and the booth started with a slight jolt.

The platform carried them along the siding loop slowly, so that it could merge smoothly onto the first track at the earliest opening. Derec's trust in the engineering job done by the robots was so great that he never worried about safety. If the robots themselves had any doubts about the system, the First Law would have forced them to keep the humans from riding in it.

He didn't know exactly how the platforms were powered, though it must have been through the tracks. In a city where construction was rampant, these details often came and went so fast that learning them just didn't matter. The platforms moved quickly, with a faint hum, and never seemed to need sudden changes in speed.

At Ariel's suggestion, they got off at a couple of tunnel stops to question more robots, but this random search continued to produce nothing. They emerged from the system as close to the Key Center as they could, but still some distance away. In order to go on questioning robots on the street, they took the slidewalk, though they did not learn anything new this way, either.

When they first came into view of the dome, Derec stopped short. A huge opening gaped in the curving surface, and gigantic pieces of machinery, some easily ten and fifteen meters high, were being driven into the dome on a flatbed vehicle. More robots were visible inside than before, possibly to install the new equipment.

"If they were people," said Derec, "I'd try to get inside during the confusion. The trouble is, I don't see any confusion. They know what they're doing. I don't think there's much point in trying to sneak in right now."

"Let's move along." She took his arm and steered him away. "No sense alerting Keymo's security to the fact that we're back."

"True."

They began to walk a discreet perimeter around the dome, making further inquiries of robots they met. The lack of information made it clear that the strangers had simply not been there.

"They will be," said Ariel. "They have to come here for the Key sooner or later. Suppose we instruct all the robots in the neighborhood to report sightings directly to us on the console."

"We can try," he said doubtfully. "The way the city keeps expanding, their population shifts all the time."

They continued their perimeter, now adding the instruction that the robots report sightings directly to them, and also to the central computer under the heading of "alien presences." When they had completed the circuit, Derec found himself gazing with hands on hips at the seamless wall of the Key Center, where the big opening was now fully sealed and scarless.

"This walking around talking just isn't getting us anywhere," Derec said. "Looking for our mysterious strangers is all right, but if we leave Robot City, we can forget about them anyhow. We can't get around it. We have to get inside the dome and get one of those keys."

"I'm afraid you're right. Look, I owe you on this one. Come on, let's do it. Do you remember where you left your boot?"

"Yeah, over there."

"You get over to it. I'm going to provide the diversion you needed the last time, over at the opposite side."

"No good. I won't know when to enter unless I can see you."

"All right—I'll stand just in sight. That way the curve of the dome will help keep the security robot from seeing you."

"Its name is Security 1K."

He walked over to the spot where a portion of his boot was still protruding from the wall, and waved to her. In response, she pounded on the wall.

"Hey! Open up in there! This is a human order!"

She did not, however, step back. With both fists on her hips and her feet wide apart, she stood with her toes right up against the wall of the dome.

The wall opened, as before, with a tearing sound right in front of her. Security 1K started to step out, but when she held her ground, the robot remained where it was. Derec could just barely see its hands moving. The robot was going to see him from that spot.

"We have learned that three other humans are present on the planet of Robot City," Ariel began. "We must speak with Keymo. These humans may endanger us."

Derec did not wait any longer. He pulled the boot just loose enough to get ahold of the free edges of dianite. When he began to pull gently, it ripped apart without much noise.

Inside the dome, everything was different. The floor was crammed with machinery, some of it even larger than the pieces he had seen entering a while before. Other units were quite compact.

He noted thankfully that the spaces between many of them offered him room to maneuver without being in anyone's line of sight, at least as long as Ariel kept Security 1K occupied. As carefully as he could, he crawled and scooted through the dark passages between machines, away from the robots he could see working here and there. This gradually moved him to a side of the building where he was able to peek out across the floor.

Now that the new machines had been installed, the crew in the dome was down to normal numbers again. They seemed more crowded in the smaller space remaining to them, but, as usual, they were efficiently concentrating on their tasks. That single-minded dedication helped Derec move unnoticed.

He caught sight of the security seat on its high perch. From where he was now, he could not see if Ariel was still keeping Security 1K busy, but that console was too inviting to pass up. Still moving cautiously, he reached the bottom of the perch.

The lift was a smaller version of those he had seen on the asteroid, and a version of the tunnel booths. A smaller lever lowered the entire seat, and, once he was in it, a button on the arm raised it. The seat moved up until it was just beneath the ceiling he had observed on his first visit. At the summit, he found himself looking out over the entire floor, with a complex array of controls and displays in front of him.

Not a single robot looked up at him. To one side, Security 1K stood with his back to the interior of the building, still talking with Ariel. Derec concentrated on the displays.

Very little of it meant anything to him. However, he was sure that the performance of every machine was being monitored here, as well as the wall of the dome. Both areas were construed as matters of security, apparently.

The console also had a computer terminal. Unlike his, this one had the VoiceCommand still hooked up. He leaned down and spoke softly.

"Central computer."

"Acknowledged." The voice was loud and made him jump.

"Lower your volume to match mine. Convert all the symbols on these monitors to full Standard terms."

A moment later, Derec was reading the monitors in amazement. As he had deduced earlier, Keymo had destroyed the Key to Perihelion in the process of having it analyzed. The robot was now overseeing the manufacture of many keys based on the same principle. The most startling monitor read, "Upper Level: Final integration of individual units and cooling. Interface with hyperspace, designated danger zone. Integration equipment producing vacuum effect of air out of dimension. Air movement, heat production, hyperspace controlled by drive unit."

He had to read it several times before he got it. The keys were being completed on the upper level in some kind of dangerous interface with hyperspace, which probably explained why it was removed from the rest of the facility. Apparently the manufacturing process created a vacuum that drew air into hyperspace.

His heart began to pound with excitement. "Where is the entrance to the upper level? And how do I get through it?"

"It opens directly above the security console. The seat will lift to that level. The dome surface can also be opened directly to and from the outside if necessary."

"Open the ceiling. This is, uh, a security matter." My security, anyway, he thought. He held his breath as he watched the ceiling. The computer assumed that the voice speaking into this console held sufficient authority to give this order, and did not require further identification. So far, the best thing about security on Robot City was its relative laxity. In a community of responsible positronic robots, the security measures had rarely been given a true challenge.

The dianite in the ceiling opened and he drove the seat on up through the hole.

CHAPTER 5

A HAND ON A KEY

Ariel had only two ideas for keeping Security 1K occupied. When it stood it front of her and started to step out, she forced herself to stand her ground. As she had expected, the influence of the First Law prevented it from forcing her aside, though in an emergency she doubted that it would have hesitated.

The robot remained just inside the dianite wall, watching her from the darkness of its horizontal eyeslit.

"I need to see Keymo," she said. All she had in mind was to present a First Law problem and to speak as slowly and as long as she could. Derec would have to do the rest by getting inside and getting a key, if he could, as quickly as possible.

"You may not enter this facility. Keymo is occupied." If possible, its voice was even more formal than the usual robot speaking voice. "May I help you?"

"This is a First Law problem." She started to say more, then remembered that she was stalling.

The robot waited until it was clear that she was not going to explain without prompting. "What is this problem?"

"A total of five humans are in Robot City."

"Yes? You are the one called Katherine?"

"I used to be. My real name is Ariel."

"Another is called Derec."

"That's right."

"What is the First Law problem?"

Ariel smiled to herself. That was the kind of stalling she wanted. What she had to do was be just a little illogical or unclear, forcing it to ask questions for clarification.

"Three other humans are here."

"Who are they?"

"We don't know."

"Who is in danger?"

"Derec and I are in potential danger."

"What danger is this?"

"Well—humans don't have to obey the First Law. So these other three could be dangerous to us."

"In what way?"

"Uh, I'm not sure."

"There is no clear danger." The robot took a step backward as a prelude to resealing the wall.

"How much experience have you had with humans?" She called quickly. "Do you know their history with each other?"

"No." It stopped where it was, now more shadowed inside the dome. "I have had only two previous experiences with a human."

"So! You don't know how they fight all the time? And have a history of wars and killing each other?"

"Some human history is available in the central computer library. In what way does this relate to the First Law problem?" The robot stepped forward again to its previous spot.

"Well, unknown humans are generally considered dangerous. You can never tell what they'll do or why."

"For what reason?"

"Just because they're unknown. We have to be careful. This is a normal part of being human, especially when you're traveling around in unfamiliar places."

"You consider unidentified humans to be dangerous until more information is available?"

"Yes! Yeah, that's it."

"No humans are in this facility. What do you need with Keymo for your First Law problem?"

"Keymo is in charge of making teleportation devices. This is the only way we know of to leave Robot City."

"You are in no clear danger. Therefore, no First Law problem pertains. Teleportation devices are not required."

"We could be killed or injured by surprise. This has happened to people many times. Your failure to help now is a First Law violation."

Ariel saw the robot hesitate, and suddenly realized that she might win this argument, let alone succeed in stalling. "Keymo is in charge of this facility, correct? Let Keymo decide."

The robot looked at her. "I am equipped to make decisions of this kind. Keymo does not have greater authority to judge and resolve a First Law problem than I have."

"So you agree that this *is* a First Law problem." She made it statement, not a question.

"That is not clear."

"But Keymo does have authority over the Key to Perihelion and the other keys. You don't have that. Since the resolution of the problem requires my getting ahold of the Key—or, keys, rather—Keymo is the one I must consult."

"You have not proven that you are in danger."

Shuddering with frustration, she drew in a long, deep breath. "Listen to me! I *believe* we may be in danger! I know a lot more about people than you do! You don't know enough about humans to judge if we're in danger!" She stared at him in fury, breathing hard.

At last the robot stepped back, making room for her. "We shall consult Keymo."

She smiled with relief and followed him inside the building. The robot led her through a winding route around machines of various sizes and types, none of which were familiar to her. She wanted to look around for Derec, but was afraid to be obvious about it. He could easily be lost among all the units here. Within the range of the cautious glances she took, he was nowhere in sight.

Keymo was standing over its console on the floor when they approached.

"This human claims to have a First Law problem," said Security 1K. "One that only you can resolve."

"You are the one called Katherine?"

"I used to be. My new name is Ariel."

"I understand. My designation was recently changed, also. What is the nature of this First Law problem?"

"Here we go again," she muttered to herself. "Look—how much do you know about human history? About how humans kill each other all the time and fight wars and stuff?"

Derec looked up apprehensively as the seat carried him into the dimmer light of the second story. He was most worried about being challenged by a robot up here, but as the seat clicked into place and the dianite solidified beneath it, he found himself standing behind a curved metal screen. On one side, pale orange light glowed from a doorway in the screen. Otherwise, the entire length of the short wall—the area with lift access—was screened off.

He slid out of the seat and carefully peeked around the edge of the doorway.

Only one robot was in the area. It stood in the foreground watching as a tray was extended toward it from inside a block housing about two meters high. The tray held an array of shining silver rectangles about five centimeters by fifteen—exactly the appearance of the original Key of Perihelion.

Derec guessed that the unit expelling the tray had just completed the final integration and cooling. As he watched, the robot picked up one key by itself and slid it into a slot in another unit. It then studied the readouts. It looked like a testing procedure.

Another wall, which sealed off the bulk of this level, was just beyond the block housing. Derec heard a muted hum from beyond it. The pale orange light was thrown by a series of monitors high on this wall, and cast a series of faint, overlapping shadows.

At the moment, he had nothing to do but watch. If his entry had been unnoticed downstairs, he was not pressed for time. Getting a key by stealth might be easier up here than by launching into another frustrating debate about the Laws.

Apparently, the entry into hyperspace was behind the big wall. It did not look especially strong, but the minimalist engineering characteristic of the Avery robots made all appearances deceiving. He would not have been surprised to find the barrier very solid and the sound beyond it absolutely deafening.

The robot took the key from the testing unit, or whatever it was, then punched a button and set it down on the tray. It stood with its back to Derec as it picked up another key and inserted it. At no time had the robot looked away from the readouts and keys, or moved its feet from their positions.

With the sound from beyond the wall as camouflage, Derec thought he just might be able to move without being noticed. He kept an eye on the robot as he slid around the edge of the doorway and crept behind it. The robot continued to watch the monitors.

The key that had already been tested glinted alone at one end of the tray. Derec stood directly behind the robot, waiting to see the robot's pattern of movement again. When the next key was ejected, the robot laid it next to the previous one and inserted a third into the unit it faced.

Derec reached very slowly for one of the tested keys, keeping his eyes on the robot for any sign of unexpected movement. The robot did not look away from the readouts. Derec picked up one of the keys and slowly began to withdraw his arm.

Just as he noticed that his arm was throwing a faint shadow across the monitors, the robot whirled and grabbed his throat in a hard squeeze. He began to choke, his tongue out and his eyes bulging.

A second later, the pressure was immediately released on his throat, but as he bent forward, gasping, the robot took a firm, though gentler, grip on his arm. He still held the key behind his back.

"Humans are more fragile than robots," said the robot apologetically. It was quivering with the internal trauma caused by a potential violation of the First Law. "I did not realize immediately that the First Law pertained. Not until I turned and saw you. You are unharmed?" Its speech was slow.

Derec nodded, swallowing. "Yeah."

The robot was still shaking and hesitant. "Identify yourself and your purpose here."

"My name is Derec. And I'm okay, so don't short-circuit yourself. Uh—"

"Security 1K did not notify me of your entry. This is a restricted area. Show your clearance."

"I don't have any. I'll just go." Derec turned, but the robot did not relinquish his arm.

"Return the key in your hand."

Derec couldn't think of an argument, so he held out the key, smiling weakly. The robot took it. Then the robot looked at a light blinking on one of the monitors.

"We shall go downstairs," it said. "I believe your presence here has been noted. In any case, that warning light summons all who are up here to report to Keymo."

"You might take a key with you." Derec reached around the robot for one. As he had expected, the robot grasped his arm. Derec feigned a shot of pain, wincing theatrically and twisting around so that he backed into the tray. As the robot pried one key out of his hand, he reached behind him with the other hand and palmed the other key that had already been tested.

Without further conversation, the robot escorted Derec around the screen to the security seat. It had Derec sit down, while it stood on some kind of bar beneath the seat. The floor opened, and they rode down together. Derec could see Security 1K standing with Ariel at Keymo's desk.

She gave him a questioning look as he was half pulled over to the console. He suppressed a smile with considerable effort. These robots were too sharp to miss any hint of collusion between them. He broke eye contact with her.

Before Keymo could speak, Derec decided to throw the robot off guard by taking the offensive.

"How did you know I was up there?"

"Both my console and the security console register heat generation and weight on each floor. However, I did not notice your presence immediately, as I had been distracted by discussions of possible imperatives under the Laws of Robotics." Keymo nodded toward Ariel and Security 1K. Then it addressed the robot still holding Derec's arm. "Process 12K, you may release your grip. Report what transpired in your jurisdiction."

"The human came up behind me and reached for one of the finished keys," said the robot from the upper floor. "He did this twice. I retrieved the key in both cases and retrieved them. When I first apprehended him, I did not know that the First Law pertained to the situation. I almost harmed him."

"We are speaking aloud for your benefit," Keymo said to Derec and Ariel. "On this matter of the First Law, you should be informed of our discussion. Derec, you are unharmed?"

"Uh, yeah. I'm okay." Derec, now free of Process 12K's grasp, moved away from him slightly. He had been feeling the key in his hand, and remembering the way it worked. Carefully, he shifted it around, pushing each corner of the key in turn. A button appeared on the last corner, on the side facing him.

Now he had to get Ariel to grip the key, or at least hold onto him, so he could push the button. With the robots so close, they wouldn't get more than one chance. Wherever the key took them would be an escape from the immediate scene; he would have to gamble that it was set for a safe place. After that, they could plan their next move.

"Ariel has claimed that a First Law problem exists," said Keymo. "Do you agree that you two are in danger from unknown humans present on the planet?"

"Uh—" Derec caught her slight nod. "Yeah. You bet. We have no idea who they are."

"Neither of you has presented any specific danger or any evidence of one," said Keymo. "Do you have any evidence of danger that she does not possess?"

"Well . . . no." Derec shrugged slightly and started shuffling his feet. He leaned a little closer to Process 12K. As he had hoped, Process 12K moved away slightly. Derec stepped in front of him, so that only Security 1K stood between Ariel and him. "I agree with her, though. People can be very dangerous —especially strangers. We would be a lot safer getting off this planet."

"You will have more contact with humans off this planet than you have here," said Keymo. "Most of them will, of course, be strangers, and therefore dangerous by your description. Here you have an entire population of robots that cannot allow you to come to harm."

"Only if you can protect us," said Ariel.

"Elsewhere," said Keymo, "you will have only yourselves to rely upon for safety."

"Now listen to her," said Derec. He reached in front of Security 1K to take her arm and pulled her to him. "The two of us are isolated here. . . ." He was just talking as a distraction, while he got an arm around her and pulled one of her arms behind her back. He placed her hand, behind both their backs, on the key with his.

"Now," he declared triumphantly, holding the key with one hand and pushing the button with the other.

Nothing happened.

CHAPTER 6
STRANGERS IN TOWN

Back in their apartment, Derec kicked the chair in front of the computer console and sent it skidding across the hard floor into the other one.

"Those filthy, stinking, walking, frosted slag heaps! What about the First Law? Doesn't that apply to the keys?"

"Apparently not," Ariel said bitterly. "If Keymo was telling the truth when he said that their keys are all initialized in that processing machine, and that they only work for the type of being that initializes them, then their keys will only work for robots. And if they initialize them by hand, that ruins them for us, too. They listened to my argument because of the First Law, not because they had keys that could send us away."

"I felt like an utter fool standing there holding that key when nothing happened. And then they scanned the wall to find out how I got in, and gave me my boot back." He looked down at the matched boots that he wore on his feet again. "You can bet the same trick won't work a second time."

"Well, at least they just threw us out. There wasn't any penalty or anything." She sighed and sat down in one of the chairs where it was, without bothering to move it back into its place.

"I was so proud of myself for talking my way in to see Keymo, too."

"The First Law did us that much good, at least." He started pacing the perimeter of the small room. "I thought we were so close to getting away from here. I thought we had it." He paused when he saw Ariel leaning forward in the chair, staring glumly at the floor.

She glanced up at him and nodded dejectedly.

"Well, look. It isn't over yet. I mean, we aren't going to give up." He sat down in the console chair and gazed at the blank screen thoughtfully. "All right. What's our next move? Let's see." He started working on the keyboard.

She watched him for a moment. "You're looking for the other humans on the planet, I suppose."

"Of course. They got here, somehow; we can leave the same way, whatever it was."

"But we haven't made any progress finding them. What else can we do?"

"We didn't really apply ourselves before. I figured Keymo was our best bet, and the other humans just a backup. Now it's time to get serious about them."

"I hope it makes a difference." Her tone was still discouraged, but she pulled her chair closer.

"I'll start with that file we had earlier," said Derec. "Hey, we're in luck."

"Really?" She looked up hopefully.

"The two strangers who are traveling together have been sighted several more times."

"What about the third?"

"No, there's no more mention of that one. I hope he's okay. I wonder if the third one is with the other two, or if they just happened to arrive about the same time."

"If they came separately, then we might have two ways to get away from Robot City."

"Good point," said Derec. "I just hope that the third one is simply hiding better than the other two."

"What do you mean?"

"If they all came together, the third one could have left again in the only transportation, whatever it is."

"Oh, Derec. Why did you have to bring that up?"

"We have to consider all the possibilities, don't we?" He

turned to look at her. "Besides, getting in touch with some people for a change is still going to be an advantage. At some point, someone will come back for them. They'll be part of the spacefaring community, at least, not like these isolationist robots."

"Suppose we try to think along that line. Do we have any way of guessing who they could be?"

"I'll enter what we have. The real problem is that we don't know the location of this planet."

"We know that Dr. Avery wanted Robot City to be away from the beaten track," said Ariel. "My mother always emphasized how eccentric he was. I'm certain we aren't near any major spacelanes."

"I don't think we're in too much of a backwater, either. If Dr. Avery was the megalomaniac you said, then at some point he probably planned to show off his success to other people."

"Mother would have wanted to see it. And, you know what? He faced a lot of skeptics on Aurora. Eventually, he'd want to prove to them that he could do what he said."

"Good. We don't have much to go on, but it's something." Derec summarized the information he read on the screen. "Aurora is probably the nearest habitable planet, and it's almost certainly the nearest planet of any significance."

"If we do get a ride out of here, that'll be convenient," she observed. "I'm willing to take small favors."

"Let me go on. The odds of three people just landing here at almost the same time purely by chance in two spacecraft are too low to think about. One spacecraft, maybe, if it had mechanical trouble or something, but not two. Assuming we are close to a spacelane, and remembering that this is all just surmise anyhow, we have to figure that our visitors came here deliberately."

"I can't honestly see why anybody would want to come here," said Ariel. "There's no business to conduct. And it's not exactly Fun City. There's no entertainment or anything."

"I know. And pioneering commercial interests would show up in force, not one or two people at a time."

"Individuals wouldn't have much of anything to do here that I can think of," she went on. "Even if I weren't sick, I'd still want to get away from here. The robots run everything on their terms."

"I think we can rule ourselves out as the reason, don't you?"

Derec asked. "As far as we know, no one has any way of knowing that either of us is here."

"Don't I know it." She shook her head in resignation, with a wistful smile.

"So that leaves Robot City itself as the reason."

"But I told you that Dr. Avery kept its location a secret. My mother was sure that was very important to him."

"You also said that he disappeared a long time ago. If he's dead, could he have left some information behind in the office that someone got? Or spilled the secret someplace else out in space before he died? And now they've used the information to come here. Or he's back himself."

"With a guy like that, anything's possible," she said reluctantly. "But it sounds out of character for him to reveal more than he wanted. Besides, any people who had learned the secret would have shown up here a long time ago."

"Not if it was well hidden. Maybe they just found it."

"Maybe. I guess." She looked at him. "Do you think it's Avery?"

"No. The sightings just aren't consistent with his ability to go into that office in the Compass Tower. Our visitors are as lost as we are. And they can get us off this rock, too."

"So much for them finding Robot City," said Ariel. "What about us finding them?"

"I wish I'd had the time to streamline the computer by now. It just isn't that reliable. If it was, we could use it to help."

"We can try, can't we? Can you give some kind of standing instruction to the robots to look for the people?"

"Yeah, I can try, but we have the same problems as before. The instructions don't reach every single robot, and they take a long time to reach a lot of them. And even that assumes Dr. Avery didn't counterprogram against it for some weird reason of his own."

She shook her head. "He was too paranoid. If he was careful enough to keep the secret of this place, I'm sure he would have approved of ordering the robots to keep watch for outsiders."

"We already know that some robots are reporting their sightings. I'll order all the robots to do that, and. . . ." he trailed off. "Well, I don't know. Maybe we're just going around in circles."

"What's wrong?"

"Well, I just don't know if it'll make a difference, like I said. It's just more of what's already in the computer."

"All we can do is give them the instruction and hope they get us some information," she said. "Then we'll try to think of something else. What's wrong with that?"

"Yeah, here goes. But what we really need is for the robots to detain them if they can, and I don't see how they can do that. That might violate the First Law."

"Wouldn't that depend on the particulars of the situation? Maybe the robots could persuade them to come. Anyway, the robots just have to avoid harming them. And they might want to see us. I guess they could bring them here, don't you?"

"I'm putting in the order. If there are any robots who can find and identify these strangers, they are to bring them here if they can. The robots can worry about the Law problems when the time comes." He sat back in his chair with a sigh. "I just don't know if any of this will make a difference."

"We've been going at this pretty hard," said Ariel. "Why don't we take a break? It's time for something to eat, anyway."

"Ugh," said Derec, and they both laughed. "All right. We'll force down anything we can stomach from the processor for lunch. After that, assuming we live, we'll probably be glad to go out and engage in endless debates with uncooperative robots."

Ariel got up, smiling. "I guess we can take our motivation wherever we find it."

After they had eaten, they ventured out once more to see if they could find some evidence of the strangers in the city. Derec started out eager and full of energy, in large part because Ariel's illness was on his mind. He wanted to make sure that she knew he wasn't dawdling.

At her suggestion, he agreed after a while to take it easy. Rushing around wasn't likely to help at this stage of the search. They had alerted the robots as much as they could, and they had a list of locations of previous sightings. Now all they could do was walk around, hoping to chance across a lead.

The worst problem was that the sightings offered no pattern that they could recognize. Since the lone traveler had not been reported at all for some time, they decided to forget about that one for the present. The sightings of the two traveling together were completely random, as far as they could tell.

The most recent sighting had taken place on the outskirts of the city. They rode the tunnels to the end of the trunkline at the edge of the city, and then had to surface. There, they managed to hitch a ride in the cab of a huge liquid transporter of some kind. They hopped off when its route diverged from theirs.

As they walked, they got their first look at the long, three-stage mole device that dug the underground tunnels and left a fully equipped, functioning platform system behind. This segment was not being used because it had not been connected to the main system elsewhere; otherwise, the mole device would have been underground and out of sight. It also simultaneously mined ores for construction and other uses, according to a foreman robot whom Derec questioned. It seemed to be a modified version of a gatelike device he had seen sifting the asteroid in search of the original Key for the Avery robots, shortly after waking up with amnesia, and the great mining and construction devices that had been crucial to the automatic shapechanging of the city.

They also saw a number of buildings under construction and some freshly finished. These included some smaller domes of bronze dianite reminiscent of the Key Center. Nowhere, however, did any of the robots remember any additional sightings of humans.

CHAPTER 7
THE CYBORG

His name was Jeff Leong. He opened his eyes in darkness and wondered where he was. At least he was alive, and not in pain.

He seemed to be lying on his back, comfortably. Pale, colored lights crossed his vision from his left, suggesting monitor readouts. He supposed they were medical equipment of some kind, and turned his head to the left, expecting it to involve considerable effort and discomfort. Instead, he moved easily and comfortably, though he found wires, now, under his cheek, that connected his head to the equipment by his side.

Dim light seemed to have come on in the room. He could see outlines in the room around him, and of course the lit displays of the monitors. The readouts meant nothing to him, though, so he straightened his head again.

He felt fine. That hardly made any sense.

Since he had only been a passenger on the spaceship *Kimbriel,* he did not have a clear understanding of the disaster. The captain had spoken over the intercom, saying that a mechanical problem had developed, and that they had left Aurora too far behind to return safely. The navigator had located a habitable planet, however, and they would attempt an emergency stop in a lifepod.

At the time, Jeff had been excited. He had had faith in the crew and had actually looked forward to an unscheduled adventure on a planet he had never seen. He assumed that was where he was now.

The door at the far end of the room opened and a robot entered. Full light came on in the room, and Jeff saw that his visitor was a blue-skinned robot of a specific type that he did not recognize. The robot walked to the monitors and studied each one carefully.

"Where am I?" Jeff asked. His voice sounded a little odd, but he had no trouble speaking.

"You are in Human Experimental Facility 1, Room 6, in Robot City," said the robot.

"Robot City? On what planet?"

"The planet is also called Robot City."

"Who are you?"

"I am Surgeon Experimental 1."

"Uh, can I see my doctor?"

"I am your doctor, along with Human Medical Research 1."

"Is he a robot, too? From his name, I suppose—"

"Yes. What is your name?"

"I'm Jeff Leong."

"Are you still in harm?"

"Huh?"

"How . . . are you? How do you feel?"

"Oh. I feel pretty good, actually. My voice sounds kind of strange, though, doesn't it?"

"It has changed. Please tell me the events leading to your arrival here."

"Our ship developed a mechanical emergency of some kind. We came here for an emergency landing, but we didn't make a very good job of it. I remember the captain warning us that it would be a hard impact."

"What other events led to your landing?"

"What other events? I don't know any other events. I was just a passenger. Look, where's everybody else?"

"I must inform you that you are the only survivor."

Jeff stared up at the ceiling, filled with many emotions. He had not expected that answer, yet he was not surprised. All the crew and passengers had been killed because of an accident—yet, he had somehow survived. It hadn't really sunk in yet. If anything, he felt more guilt than sorrow.

"Were you traveling with family or friends?"

"No," he murmured softly. "No, I didn't know anybody on board."

"What was your destination?"

"Mine, personally? Well, I was leaving home for college. I'm from Aurora."

"You were not coming to Robot City?"

"Not deliberately, no. Not until the ship malfunction." Jeff looked up at him. "Do you know what happened to it?"

"The mother ship exploded outside the atmosphere. The life-pod you were riding with the other passengers crashed in its attempt to land."

"I guess I lucked out, huh? I feel okay."

"I have summoned Research 1, the other member of the Human Experimental Team. We shall explain together. Perhaps you did luck out, as you put it. You say you feel well?"

"Yeah. Can I get up?"

"Have you observed yourself?"

"No . . . why, was I scarred or something?" Jeff put a hand to his face, and felt a hard, unfamiliar surface. "Am I in a mask? Bandages or something?"

Surgeon 1 paused as another robot entered the room. "This is Human Medical Research 1. Our patient is named Jeff Leong."

"Hi," Jeff said cautiously.

"Hi," said Research 1, in exactly the same tone. "Surgeon 1, how do the monitors read?"

"They indicate, taken together, an excellent condition."

Surgeon 1 walked up and looked down at Jeff, who felt cowed by the unequal numbers and strange appearances. He would have preferred a human doctor.

"Do you feel excellent?" Surgeon 1 asked.

"Well, yeah, but I feel all mummified or something. What happened to me?"

Research 1 moved to the foot of the bed and looked at him

straight on. "Since the experiment has succeeded, I believe we can tell you with a minimum of shock. You may sit up."

"Uh, okay." Jeff expected to be helped, as solicitous doctors and nurses tended to do, but the robots remained where they were. He sat up, quite easily, watching Research 1's careful study of the monitors. Then he looked down and saw the blue-skinned texture of his own legs.

At first, he simply didn't understand. He wondered why his legs were encased in this stuff. When he reached out to touch one of his legs, he saw his hand and arm for the first time, made of the same unfamiliar blue substance. Then, suddenly understanding what had happened, he looked at his other robotic arm and then down at his chest. In growing panic, he clapped his blue hands against his torso and then ran them across the new contours of his face.

"The monitors read properly," said Research 1. "All evidence so far indicates a successful procedure. You are, of course, emotionally agitated. This reaction is also occurring normally."

Jeff collapsed back on the bed. The monitor lights jumped as they noted the impact. "I'm a robot. I can't believe this. I'm a *robot.*"

"We wish you to understand something," said Surgeon 1. "The First Law required this development, under the circumstances of our finding you."

"What? How? How could the First Law require this? You don't think this has harmed me? I'm a person, not a robot!" Jeff started to sit up again, but really didn't feel like rising. He was not tired, or physically weak, but he didn't want to move, as though he might somehow injure himself in this alien body.

"You were injured when we found you," said Research 1. "We do not have knowledge here of human thoracic and abdominal organs. Our medical library is inconsistent and uneven. However, we had some experimental information regarding the frontier of knowledge about the human nervous system. Since we could not allow you to come to further harm if we could prevent it, we were forced to use our experimental knowledge in preserving you as a living entity."

"I'm not sure I follow you," Jeff whispered. "Say it out straight, will you?"

"We have transplanted your brain into one of our humanoid robot bodies because we could not repair yours."

Jeff closed his eyes and lay still for a moment. When he opened them, he stared morosely at Research 1. "What happened to my body?"

"It has been frozen. We believe, with our limited information, that it is actually not injured beyond repair. We do not, however, know how to fix it. Do you have medical knowledge that could assist us in repairing your body?"

"Me? I'm just a kid on his way to college—a teenager. I don't know anything about that. At least, not on the level you would need."

"We assembled this team specifically for this project," said Surgeon 1. "We are not aware of other successful transplants of the same type."

"Great," Jeff said sarcastically. "I guess."

"You do not seemed pleased with this success," observed Surgeon 1. "Do you disbelieve that this is the least harm to you that we could arrange under the circumstances?"

"No . . . no, I don't disbelieve you. I just . . . don't want to be a robot!" He sat up this time and yanked the monitor wires free of himself. "Don't you get it? I'm not me anymore! I'm not Jeff Leong."

The robots made no move.

"That is not entirely true," said Research 1. "Your identity resides in your brain. Unless the trauma of the crash caused you to lose some memory, your identity is unchanged."

"But I'm not *me*—I mean, on the outside. I don't look like this." He held up his hands, open, and shook them at the robots.

"In many ways," said Surgeon 1, "your new robot body is more efficient than your human body. It can be repaired virtually forever, provided your brain is undamaged. Only your brain will age, and it will receive the optimum support in nutrition and intrabody care. You are stronger, and your sensors are much more efficient than your former sense organs."

"Some consolation. How long do I have to stay here?"

"Your robot body is in fine condition. You are not confined to bed," said Surgeon 1. "Some simple motor tests will tell us whether all the connections from your brain to the body are correct. Please stand."

Jeff cautiously swung his legs over the edge of the bed and got up. "No problem so far."

"Place your heels together, angle your feet away from each other, and tilt your head back. Now extend your arms out straight. One at a time, touch your hands to your nose."

Jeff complied.

"Very well," said Surgeon 1. "Research 1?"

"According to the monitors, the robot body is functioning properly. We will need more space for my tests of gross motor skills. I suggest we introduce him to the exterior of this building."

Jeff walked out of the room with them and down a hallway, feeling not clumsy, exactly, but just a little too tall and too heavy. Outside, he was nearly blinded at first, but adjusted immediately. Surgeon 1 saw him flinch.

"Your eyes see a wider range of the spectrum than your human eyes did. The same will be true of your other sensors. What you just experienced was an automatic dimming of your robot eyes to allow you to see comfortably. You did just the opposite when you woke up in near darkness a little while ago."

"Excellent," said Research 1. "You are responding automatically, then. I have only a few more tests."

"Before we do that," said Jeff, "I just thought of something. What am I going to *do?*"

"Whatever you wish," said Research 1. "We have no requirements, other than those imposed on us by the Laws and by our programming. That involves our society here, not you."

"But . . . what about college? I can't go like this. . . . They won't even know who I am! I don't look like Jeff Leong any more—I don't have retinal prints, fingerprints, any kind of identifying mark."

"If your brain waves are on record anywhere, they will serve," said Surgeon 1. "However, we do not have any spacecraft available for you, anyway."

Jeff whirled on him. "You mean I'm *stuck* here?"

"We do not have spacecraft available," Research 1 affirmed.

"But . . . wait a minute! I can't stay here!"

"We have no hold on you," said Research 1. "If we ever develop the means to repair your human body and reverse the transplant, we will do so. Should spacecraft become available, travel will also be open to you."

"But I can't stay here. There's nothing to do here!"

"Please remain calm. After testing your gross motor skills, I will introduce you to the robot in charge of assigning tasks in Robot City. Perhaps you will find an activity that you will enjoy."

"Hey, now wait a minute." Jeff backed away from Research 1, and found the other two robots grasping his arms. "Hey!" He twisted, stepped sideways, and yanked his arms free. "Lemme alone."

"We must conduct more tests to measure your welfare," said Research 1.

"Look, I just—let go!" Jeff pulled his arm away from Surgeon 1 again. "Listen to me! I'm human—I'm telling you to leave me alone. Second Law, remember?" he started walking backward, awkwardly on his new legs, keeping an eye on them.

"We cannot allow you to harm yourself," Surgeon 1 reminded him. "The First Law outweighs the Second. Come back." He started for Jeff.

Jeff spun around and started running.

He found himself running down a broad thoroughfare nearly empty of vehicular traffic. Some robot pedestrians moved out of his way. He had no idea where he was going, but he wanted to think, and to do it alone.

He could hear two sets of footsteps pounding after him—and was surprised to realize that his robotic hearing was so acute that he could actually distinguish the two separate pairs of robot feet. They were calling after him, not shouting angrily the way people would, but yelling that he was still experimental, that he might harm himself, that he had to stop. He didn't stop, though; their voices simply spurred him on.

Other robots were listening, however, and trying to block his path. He dodged a couple of them and burst through the outstretched arms of several more. They all gave chase, presumably responding to the calls of the medical team that he might violate the First Law. The other robots apparently would help catch him first if they could, and worry about explanations later.

He rounded a corner without slowing down and started up a small side street. Even now, he could feel that he was running more comfortably than he had just moments before. His robot body responded quickly, and well. It had not been designed for footraces, but it was powerful and efficient. As he got more used to it, he began to turn up the speed and to hurdle minor obstacles.

Unfortunately, of course, his pursuit was all robots, as well.

He kept running.

CHAPTER 8

HITTING THE STREETS

Derec and Ariel stopped to rest on a small ridge of soil on the side of yet another construction site. As near as they could tell, the urban area of Robot City was expanding in all directions from its center, and they had been walking the perimeter of construction so they could question the robots they encountered. So far, they had traveled only a very small arc of the entire circle.

"This isn't doing us any good," Derec complained. He lay down on the dirt and leaned back against the slope.

"What isn't?" She looked carefully to make sure the slope behind here was smooth, then also leaned back. "Resting here or asking around?"

"Both, now that you mention it. But I meant asking robots at random like this. There are thousands of them, and they aren't very observant of their surroundings unless it's part of their job. They concentrate on their own tasks too much."

"I haven't thought of anything better." She closed her eyes. "My feet hurt. I'm not used to walking so much."

"I haven't thought of anything else, either. There must be something, though." He looked across the way, where a foreman robot was overseeing a large function robot of some kind. "Everything is so carefully organized. Nothing is wasted."

As they watched, the function robot raised an arm with a nozzle on the end and began to spray a heavy, viscous liquid onto the bare, level ground in front of it. Even after the liquid had landed, it swirled and shifted and moved in active currents beyond those in motion by the pressure at the nozzle. As the spray continued, the liquid formed a flat floor and then began to grow walls up from the floor, leaving space for a doorway.

Ariel opened her eyes. "Did you ask that one robot earlier how the spray works? I went to talk to another one and didn't hear your conversation."

"Yeah. I didn't understand the details, but apparently the molecules are all coded. They know where to go, and slide around in liquid form until they reach the right spot. Then they bond with their right neighboring molecules."

"Just the way this whole city works," said Ariel. "Except for us and our visitors. We don't fit. That's one thing we have in common with them, no matter who they are."

"You think it over," Derec said wearily. "Here comes another transport vehicle of some kind. I can see a humanoid riding in it. I guess I'll go interrupt its day and ask it the usual questions."

He got to his feet, and realized as he walked through a scrap area that his own legs did not have much more energy left, either. Most of the scrap was in huge, carefully stacked piles, but here and there individual pieces had fallen or been laid out to start a new stack. He noted with a mixture of interest and annoyance that none of the parts were recognizable. These Avery robots had an extremely ingrown technology.

Derec had learned how to shortcut this process somewhat. He first called out that he was human to get the robot's attention, and then ordered it to stop. In turn, the humanoid robot ordered the function robot—the transport—to stop. This time, Derec's questions paid off.

"I have seen two non-indigenous beings recently," said the robot, looking down at Derec from the high cab of the transport.

"Identify," Derec ordered, with excitement.

"I am Class 9 Vehicle Foreman 214."

"What did they look like? What were they doing?"

"One was a robot that did not respond to my communication greeting. Apparently he was on a different frequency or malfunctioning. Also, his dimensions and proportions were not quite familiar."

"What about the other one?"

"I did not see the other one clearly. It appeared to be no longer than a meter. This is an approximation. It had four extremities."

"A kid," said Derec. "A robot and a little kid. That's weird. . . . Did you speak with them?"

"No. They departed when I approached."

"What were they doing when you first saw them?"

"Walking."

"Did you hear them speak? Or have any contact with robots of any kind?"

"No."

"Say—why did you try to communicate with them?"

"Because of their unusual appearance. I thought that if the robot required assistance to a repair facility, I would offer it."

"Did you report the sighting to the central computer?"

"Yes."

"When and where did it take place?"

"Two days ago. The time—"

"That's good enough. Where?" Derec grinned. The sighting was not one of those he had found listed in the computer. Ariel came up to join them as Class 9 Vehicle 214 gave him the city coordinates of the sighting. Then the robot went on its way.

"It's a start," Derec said happily. "The sighting is two days old, but it's solid."

He filled her in on the details.

"A babysitter and a kid, maybe," said Ariel. "They might have been ejected from a lifepod in a ship emergency, or something like that. But with the transportation in this city, they could be anywhere by now."

"We have to start somewhere. Come on." Derec started in the direction of the nearest thoroughfare back toward the heart of the city.

Ariel hurried after him. "It just doesn't seem like much to go on. They must be long gone from there."

"Oh, come on! After all this time, this is the best lead we have. Why do you want to be so pessimistic?"

"It's not that, exactly."

"Then what?" He demanded angrily. "Don't you want to get away from here? Would you rather just give up?"

"Of course not! I didn't say that."

"Well, then, come on." Derec stalked along, his upbeat mood lost. The worst part of it was his realization that she was right. Their lead out here on the fringe of the city had come to nothing; chasing a two-day-old sighting might be just as hopeless.

They marched in silence for a while, then topped on the edge of the avenue. Traffic here would be nonexistent until the next construction transport was ready to head into the city again. The trips were carefully planned and maintained, as the robots were too efficient to waste any fuel or time on unnecessary runs.

After Derec had cooled down a little, he said, "Maybe these two sightings do tell us something. I think our visitors landed outside the city and entered in search of, I don't know—food and shelter, I suppose. The sighting on the fringe, here, was older. So if they went into the middle of the city for a reason, they may stay there."

"It's still a very big city," Ariel said doubtfully. Suddenly, she gasped. "That's it, Derec. What are they going to eat?"

"Well—I guess they'll get a chemical processor from the robots. . . ."

"But will they know that? Will they know to ask? Besides, the robots wanted you to solve a mystery for them, so we had special consideration."

"Maybe, but if the robots learn of the problem, the First Law will make them help out." He was stung by the fact that he hadn't thought of this himself. "Yeah, this must be the only city to be found anywhere that doesn't have a single restaurant or anything like that."

"This is our first real lead," said Ariel with a new excitement. "Once we get back to the tunnel system, let's split up. I'll follow up on our latest sighting and see if I can find a food source around there."

"Why? I thought you didn't consider that lead worth much."

"Oh, Derec, stop griping. You need to get back on the computer and see if you can locate food sources through it. This way we can cover two leads at once, that's all."

"Well, I can't argue with that. Come to think of it, if they haven't found any food, they could be in bad shape by now. We don't want them dying on us." He waved for her to follow him, pressed by a new sense of urgency.

"We can't walk all the way to the tunnel stop," she said, but she was smiling. "It's good to see the old enthusiasm back."

They actually walked some distance before a vehicle came by to give them a ride, but the walk paid off. The vehicle had departed from somewhere within the construction perimeter and would not have passed them out there. As Ariel had suggested, they split up in the tunnel system. He returned home to their computer console, while she went on to the site that Class 9 Vehicle 214 had reported.

Derec sat down at the console, glad to have another approach to use; but he hadn't forgotten that this report had been lost somewhere in the system. He started by calling up a list of stores that were edible to humans. The only inventory was in the tank of their chemical processor, according to the screen. So either the visitors were getting hungry, or they had a food source not recorded this way.

Next, he called up other materials that had been converted to edible form. Again, everything was accounted for. He asked if another chemical processor had been made or requested. Nothing like that had been recorded.

As far as Derec knew, Robot City did not have any animal life that could be caught and eaten, even by the most desperate humans. Perhaps a very talented human could build a chemical processor without the help of the robots, but it would still require parts. Nor could it produce any food without raw materials of some kind.

On the assumption that the visitors had landed outside the city and entered the perimeter where he and Ariel had first gone, he narrowed the focus of his requests and asked again if any robots in that area had sighted the strangers. Nothing turned up that way. He got the same result when looking for a record of their landing.

The only certainty Derec had was that the computer was unreliable. The answers about the chemical processor and the foodstuffs might be accurate, but the visitors were here, and that meant they had landed somewhere on the planet in a spacecraft that could, in all probability, lift off again. There had to be some way to track them.

He couldn't think of anything. With a sigh, he got up and paced idly around the small room. So far, the computer hadn't helped any this time; he wished he had gone with Ariel.

He doubted she was in much danger, especially if the visitors were a robot and a small child. Besides, he knew she could take care of herself pretty well. His attitude toward her had changed, though, ever since he had learned of the seriousness of her illness. She didn't seem quite so intimidating any more, though she was still older and more self-assured than he was. Ever since the day she had told him of the severity of her disease, and had cried in his arms, he had felt a growing protectiveness toward her.

She seemed to be okay now, though. He figured she might just laugh if he tried to tell her how he felt.

His jaw muscles tightened with the determination to prove what he could do with the computer. He sat down again and started calling up everything he could think of regarding space: records of astronomical observations, spacecraft landings, lift-offs, fly-bys . . . what else?

The computer gave him nothing on recent soft landings of spacecraft, or crashes. Nor had there been any reported sightings of landed spacecraft. Astronomical observations had not recorded any craft in orbit, either. He had to assume that either the sensors had failed in some way, or that the information was simply lost in the computer.

Food, he thought. The visitors required nutrition. That was still the best lead he had, if he could only think of a way to exploit it.

Ariel walked out of the tunnel stop and located the coordinates of the last sighting of the visitors without any trouble. Her only problem was what to do next. She was in the middle of the city, standing still as a moderately heavy traffic of robots passed her, either on slidewalks or in vehicles.

"Well, what would I do for food here?" she asked herself out loud. "Ask around, I suppose."

As always, the robots were moving with their single-minded

deliberation. The bland buildings reflected that attitude in their austere efficiency of design. No stranger, she reflected, would expect to find food in this neighborhood.

She stopped the nearest robot passing, by calling out, "I am a human who needs questions answered. Stop."

The robot stopped.

"Have you seen a robot traveling with a human child?"

"No."

"Do you know where I might find food?"

"Food. This is the energy source for humans, is it not?"

"Yes. It must be provided in a certain chemical form."

"I am not familiar with it. I do not know where to locate any. Are you in urgent need of energy?"

"I'm not," said Ariel, "but I think a small human in the company of a certain robot probably is. Almost definitely. I need to find them before the child starves. That is, runs out of energy."

"This constitutes a First Law requirement, then. I will help you search for them."

"Identify." Ariel suddenly realized that this argument could be used to harness every robot in Robot City.

"I am Courier Foreman 189."

"You supervise couriers? What do they do?"

"Couriers are function robots that carry small items to specific locations. Objects and distance vary."

"All right. Listen. You don't have to interrupt your work at all. Just spread the word to other humanoid robots as you go about your duties that a First Law problem requires their aid in locating a human child in the company of a robot, and also another human wandering around by himself."

"Understood."

"And tell them not to include me—I'm Ariel Welsh—or Derec."

"Understood. I will contact other robots through my comlink."

"Good! I have to tell Derec about this right away." Ariel turned and ran for the tunnel stop.

CHAPTER 9
JUST ONE OF THE CROWD

Jeff decided, after numerous glances back over his shoulder, that he had finally lost his pursuit. He had run blindly, turning corners and dodging behind robots and vehicles and buildings every time he could, before slowing down. He was not out of breath, or even tired, but he was disoriented and scared.

He didn't know where he was going, or even why he had run. Right now, he just wanted to be alone. He eyed warily other robots that he passed, but they paid him no particular attention. Either the medical staff had not yet put any word out, or his physical traits carried no designation they could use to identify him. The thought that he would not have to run every minute bolstered his spirits a little. The total lack of humans dampened them again.

The entire situation just didn't seem real. It was absurd. How could he, Jeff Leong, eighteen years old, recently accepted into college, a healthy and fairly normal Auroran . . . be a *robot?*

He walked. He walked straight, turned corners and then found a slidewalk and got on it. With nowhere to go and nothing to do, he just kept walking along the slidewalk.

At first, his senses were still askew. His eyes were not only more sensitive than before, but they seemed to see in a much wider range of the spectrum. He found himself looking at colors, as he termed them, that he had never seen before and had no name for—and they unnerved him. Gradually, he learned to shut out most of the unwanted light waves. The same had occurred with his hearing. It had been so acute at first that all sounds had reached him in a kind of jumble. Then he had been able, by concentrating, to reduce his hearing acuity to a level that felt comfortable. He had been intrigued by the added abilities, but he would have to learn how to control them.

The walking also helped him become more familiar with his new body. It responded smoothly and efficiently, with good balance and control. He couldn't complain about that. Before long, he had concluded that he was moving enough like the other robots, the real ones, to escape notice.

He also looked over the robots he passed, as nonchalantly as he could, in search of identifying marks. The robots bore differences, certainly, especially where job-related equipment was concerned on the non-humanoid ones. He saw several distinct but subtle pattern differences repeated on many of the humanoid robots, and guessed they represented minor engineering improvements on robots that had been made or repaired at different times. If they had individual identification, however, he was too much of a stranger here to see it.

Gradually, he found himself moving in a consistent direction. The population seemed denser that way, perhaps toward the center of the urban area. All the robots seemed intent on their own occupations, and he grew more confident that he could lose himself in the crowd.

Yet, he still had nothing to do and nowhere to go.

Ahead of him, through a crowd of robots, he thought he saw a girl, or young woman, emerge from some kind of underground entrance. With a surge of excitement, he quickened his pace and leaned to one side to look between two other robots. When they glanced at him, he straightened in alarm.

He could see her walking the other way. If he wanted to avoid notice, he would have to act with the same deliberate manner as all the robots around him. He lengthened his stride and gave chase without otherwise altering his body language.

Not far ahead, she had stopped to speak to a robot. Jeff

slowed down as he approached, and stopped when her back was to him. He was a good distance away by human standards, but after a moment of effort, he was able to sharpen his hearing enough to eavesdrop.

"Identify yourself," she was saying.

"I am Tunnel Foreman 41," said the robot.

"I'm Ariel. Please spread the word about the First Law obligation I've described."

"I must," said Tunnel Foreman 41.

The robot departed and Ariel started to go. Then she saw Jeff watching her, and she paused.

"The First Law?" Jeff asked. He wanted to continue his masquerade as a robot until he knew something about her.

"Yes," said Ariel. "We're looking for two people who are probably starving in Robot City. One is a child traveling with a robot and the other is alone. The First Law requires that all robots help locate them."

"Of course," said Jeff, suddenly realizing that of course this did not apply to him. He still had his human brain, and the imperative of the Laws was located in the positronic brains of the robots. Yet if he revealed this, his identity would be known to anyone aware of the transplant and his subsequent escape.

"Report any sightings of them to the central computer," Ariel went on. "Detain them if you can, without violating the Laws. We'll see that they're fed."

"I understand," said Jeff. He was trying frantically to think of a question, anything, to learn more about her without giving himself away.

"Identify," she said.

"Uh—Tunnel Foreman 12." He couldn't risk making up a job, in case she would recognize the fraud. "Do you know who they are?"

"Why, no." She looked at him in some surprise. "They just seem to have landed and walked into the city. In fact, if you come across them, find out what you can about their spacecraft."

"Find out what?"

"Well, where it is, if it's damaged, what kind it is. . . ." She cocked her head to one side. "None of the other robots have asked these questions."

Jeff felt the impulse to run wash over him again, but he couldn't afford to look like a fugitive. He forced himself to remain where he was, searching for something to say.

"Tell me why your responses are different."

He knew why she had changed her observation to an instruction. Now he, under the Second Law, was required to answer, or else blow his cover if he didn't. The scarcity of humans in this weird place—the only fact about it that he was sure of—would mean he wouldn't have to go through this very often.

"I cannot judge the responses of others," he said, picking his phrases carefully. "My responses are based on a desire to elicit further information that may be of help."

"Well, all right." She seemed to accept that.

To forestall another question, he asked one of his own. "What is the importance of the spacecraft?"

"It may well be the only functioning spacecraft on the planet. That's if it works at all. Now, I have to report some information. You go spread the word, all right?" She gave a little wave and walked away.

Jeff was aching to follow her, but he didn't dare act any more out of character for a robot than he had already. He watched her until she had turned a corner, then hurried to the corner and watched her departing form as the crowd of robots between them gradually closed her from his view. At least he had had some human contact; she hadn't been bad-looking, either.

He definitely wanted his human body back.

That spacecraft might mean something to him. It was a way to get off the planet, but he couldn't see leaving without his body—and he'd better be in his body at the time, since these robots might be the only ones who could manage the transplant back into it. Then, belatedly, he remembered what the medical team had told him: they needed information about human organs. Ariel's were presumably in good shape, and could act as a model.

He started briskly in the direction she had gone, now more willing to risk revealing himself . . . In sudden puzzlement, he frowned—at least inwardly. He had no idea what his robot face was doing.

The point was, what had *he* been doing? Why had he run like that from the medical team? They had just wanted to test him some more. Why had he been so secretive? Maybe Ariel would have been glad to help. He hadn't even thought of that. He had been in a fog ever since waking up.

He couldn't see her ahead anymore, but—

A hand on his shoulder startled him. He twisted away from the contact, backing toward the wall of a building. A robot had just caught up with him from behind.

"Identify yourself," said the robot. "I am Pavement Maintenance Foreman 752."

"Uh—Tunnel Foreman, uh, 12."

"Tunnel 12, is your comlink malfunctioning? I tried to contact you several times as you were standing still. You did not respond."

"No, I didn't . . . receive you."

"I am informing you so that you can report to a repair facility. However, I initially tried to contact you to say that a First Law problem has developed over the matter of two humans in Robot City."

"I am aware of it," Jeff said warily.

"Excellent. I notice that your speech pattern is also hesitant. This symptom may be related to your comlink malfunction. I will escort you to the nearest repair facility, lest you be incapacitated by an additional symptom."

"Oh—no, uh, I can find it." Jeff backed along the wall. "Thanks, anyway."

"Tunnel Foreman 12, your behavior also suggests further malfunctions. I will escort you. You are going the wrong way."

Jeff turned and began walking quickly away. "Third Law violation!" cried the robot behind him. "You must not allow harm to yourself!"

Jeff heard the footsteps behind him start to run, and took off himself. Ahead of him, robots walking his way suddenly fixed their vision on him, and acted in concert to block the way. Pavement Maintenance Foreman 752 was obviously sending out comlink signals to every robot in the vicinity.

One of those openings leading underground stood just ahead on the left. Two robots blocked his way near it. He ran toward them and feinted forward, as though he was about to leap on them. They stiffened reflexively for the impact, and he dodged into the underground opening.

He found himself running down a ramp, and nearly lost his balance when his weight on the ramp activated it. It carried him down at a quick speed, and when he recovered his footing, he ran down to the level of the tunnel platforms. He understood their purpose without a pause, since robots were speeding by on them, but he stepped into the first booth without knowing how to operate it. It started anyhow, so he was content to look back and see a number of robots in pursuit entering booths behind him.

The controls seemed to have both voice activation and key code capabilities, but he didn't now how the stops were numbered, or named, or whatever. Nor did he know anything about the layout of the city, so one stop was as good as another. His pursuit certainly knew exactly how to operate these things.

"Speed up," he said experimentally. The platform did speed up, though not greatly. It was approaching the one just ahead, and clearly would not get too close. At least the robots pursuing him could not really get their hands on him here, either. They could only follow him, and try to jump him when he got off. . . .

Unless they could get the system shut off on some emergency basis.

They'll never get me, Jeff thought firmly. Once he was out of the tunnels again, he should have one advantage: these robots, despite their equal strength and reflexes, were unaccustomed to physical conflict. He was sure his feint had succeeded for that reason; they still expected him to act logically, like a robot, even if he had "malfunctioned."

He could stop them cold if he revealed that he was human. They would have no right to harm his robot body under the First Law, then, and under the Second, they would have to obey him. Revealing himself would risk capture by the medical team, though, which he could not accept.

He shook his head, then, unsure of why he couldn't accept that. They were dangerous to him, threatening . . . for some reason. In any case, they wouldn't get him.

"Stop at the next stopping place," he said to the booth.

His platform duly routed into the next available loading loop, and he quickly hopped out. This time he was ready for the moving ramp, and ran up it even as it carried him. Up on the street again, he found the number of robots very sparse, which was just as well. Any moment, the robots pursuing him would order them to join the chase.

He ran around a corner so that he would not be immediately visible when the pursuit poured out of the tunnel stop. A large door of some kind, apparently to accommodate sizable transports, was in front of him. He started to reach for the control panel to one side of the door, then realized that a work crew was almost certainly inside. The pursuit was sure to see him any second. He looked around frantically.

In the wall next to the door, he saw a broad, round opening with a closed iris cover. The cover opened at his touch, and the smells from within told him it was a trash chute. He slid into it feet first, face down, pressing his arms and legs against the slick sides of the chute to prevent himself from shooting down into the receptacle.

The cover irised shut over his head, so he concentrated on his hearing. Footsteps sounded nearby, hesitated, shuffled, and pounded on. No voices were used; they were communicating through their comlinks. He waited, in case more were coming.

He could smell faint oils, oxidized metals, and some mild odors he could not recognize. His human nose would probably not have smelled anything. Apparently, robots produced only inorganic waste, sparing him the strong and foul odors of organic decomposition.

He was not getting tired, exactly, but he was somehow aware of unusual energy expenditure—which meant the same thing, in a way. When he had heard no sound of any robots for several minutes, he touched open the cover and pulled himself out. As before, the block was empty.

"Fooled 'em," he said aloud with a certain satisfaction. He strolled to the corner and looked up and down the street. A few robots were walking about, but traffic was very light. "Okay, gang. Now for the big test. Can you recognize me again, or not?"

As he walked, he closely eyed the robots he passed. None seemed to have any concern with him. If he possessed no external identifying mark, then his pursuit had permanently lost him when they had lost sight of him. He was comlink-invisible; not only was he incapable of receiving those signals, but he could not be tracked down by any careless broadcasting on his part. Use of the comlink would also explain why the robots found identifying marks unnecessary.

He was lost in the crowd.

Jeff smiled, at least inwardly, at the thought.

Aurora had been settled primarily by the descendants of Americans from Earth. His own ancestors had been Chinese Americans; a number of such families had been scattered about on Aurora, but they were a modest percentage of the population. Jeff had grown up knowing that he was visibly distinct anywhere he went, and he had expected the same when he went off to college—though now he was no longer sure he was going to make it.

For the first time, he resembled everyone else on the planet where he lived. It was a new experience—practically a new concept to go with his new existence. His life as a robot could be completely different for this reason, as well as for the obvious physical change.

He had to do something with himself in this new body and in this new life, such as it was. It was too soon to know what, yet, but one fact was clear: no one knew what he looked like anymore; no one could catch him. . . .

Perhaps he could make something of this new-found anonymity.

CHAPTER 10
BACON

Derec ran his hand through the bristly hair on the side of his head and stared morosely into the screen. Maybe he was just too worn out to concentrate any more. He hoped that was the problem. If not, then the reason he couldn't think of anything else to try with the computer was that he had already tried everything. He straightened in surprise when Ariel burst into their quarters.

"How did it go?" He looked up hopefully.

"I got us some help for a change," she said brightly. "As soon as I run to the personal, I'll tell you about it."

He felt a kind of disappointment that he didn't have any good news to report, but waited patiently until she had returned.

"You got us some help? Who is it? How'd you manage that?" He tried to cover his envy.

"I was talking to one of the robots, and the argument just came to me. I told a couple of them that there were humans lost in Robot City who were starving. That gave them a First Law imperative to help." She fell into her chair with a sigh. "I've been on my feet enough for one day. But at least I accomplished something out there."

"Good job," he conceded. He sat back from the console, glad for an excuse to quit for a while. "But what about their regular duties? Didn't they resist leaving them?"

"I just told them to continue their duties, and to keep an eye out for the human visitors while they did. Oh, and for them to pass the word on to other robots, of course."

"Yeah, that's a good idea. That way they don't feel a conflict between their duties and a rather vague First Law obligation."

"Did you tell them to report to the central computer?"

"Of course. But, uh. . . ." She inclined her head toward his console with a pointed smile. "As I recall, your department hasn't been exactly on top of everything."

"Yeah, I know. Whether it gets on record where I can find it is an open question." Derec acknowledged the point with an embarrassed shrug. "At least it improves our chances."

"Anyway, I wanted to tell you about the new First Law argument right away. With the robots helping us search, we don't have to do the legwork any more. Have you gotten anywhere?"

"Yeah—well, no, not really." He sighed and looked wearily at the screen. "I've eliminated a number of areas as having no source of food. As near as I can tell, the only place to find edible plants and other plants with processible content is the reservoir area. They haven't been sighted anywhere in that direction at all."

"Maybe we should go out that way ourselves, and give this First Law argument to the robots working there, just in case."

"I guess it couldn't hurt. At the moment, I'm too tired to plan strategy."

"We can do some more planning tomorrow. What else have you figured out? Or is that it?"

"No, that isn't it," he growled. "I'm sure now that the only chemical processors are ours, and the one that the robots used to feed us when we first arrived. Before, it was just a good surmise. Now I'm certain."

"Where does that leave us now?"

Derec stifled a yawn and looked at the clock. "It leaves me beat, for one thing." *And too worn out to argue,* he thought to himself as he shut off the console.

"It's not that late, but I'm worn out, too. Besides, with the robots contributing, there's a chance something will happen even if we aren't killing ourselves every second."

"I'm going to eat and then go collapse." Derec got up and punched a code into the chemical processor. "Want anything?"

"As much as I'd rather not, I guess I'd better. I'm so sick of all the stuff it makes. I guess it doesn't even matter very much what it is. Make it two of whatever you're having, okay?"

"Coming right up."

She was walking toward him when she suddenly gasped and bent forward at the waist, her eyes bulging, clutching her abdomen with one arm.

He moved quickly to catch her by the shoulders. Gently, he eased her into a chair. "What is it? Can I do anything?"

"No," she whispered hoarsely. She was still doubled over. "Just give me a minute, okay?" Her eyes were fixed on the floor in front of her as she held her position. She had broken out in a sweat, and her face was pale.

He backed up a little, but remained standing, watching her apprehensively. When the processor buzzed that their late meal was ready, he took out the plates and set them down. He sat down in his chair, trying not to make her more self-conscious than she already was, but he was too worried to start eating.

Finally, she straightened and drew in a deep breath. "I'm okay," she said weakly. "Really." Her face was shiny with sweat. "It's passing. Go ahead and eat. Don't wait for me."

He tried to phrase his question carefully. "Could it be something, uh, ordinary?"

"Sure." She forced a faint smile. "It was just a dizzy spell. I'm worn out from running around all day. Besides, I haven't eaten enough today. That's all it is."

Derec nodded. Neither of them believed it, but they couldn't do anything about her disease, anyway. Stating the obvious wouldn't accomplish anything. A feeling of helplessness kept him just sitting there, looking at her.

After a moment, she reached for her plate, and they ate in silence.

He did not go to bed right away, after all. Instead, he kept thinking of little chores to do, cleaning up and pacing about, for as long as she remained up. He wanted to be on hand if she had another dizzy spell, but she seemed all right.

Finally, she retired, probably sensing that he was going to

stay up as long as she did. He went to bed, but worry kept him awake for some time. As he lay in the dark, the terrible puzzle kept taunting him: at least one spacecraft had landed somewhere on the planet, but they could find no way to locate it. And if they couldn't get Ariel to medical help of some kind, somewhere. . . .

He refused that line of speculation. *How* could they find the spacecraft; that was the question. He turned over restlessly, gradually starting to doze and to dream of vague shadowy figures running away down the fast lane of the slidewalks, always just out of reach, agile and elusive despite their imminent starvation.

The next morning he awoke to a pleasant, familiar, salty aroma drifting in from the other room. Could their chemical processor have produced that? He could hear Ariel moving about, and got up full of curiosity. When he opened his door, she was standing at the chemical processor, just turning to face him.

"Look what I managed to get out of this thing," she said with a smile, holding out a plate.

Derec took one of the long, flat strips from it and bit off the end. "Mmm—bacon!"

"Simulated bacon, anyway. Healthier than the real thing, probably. I've been up for hours, and thought I'd try experimenting with the processor." She laughed. "I've had the recycler going all morning with my failures. So far, this is the best improvement on what we've been eating."

"It's great. Practically got me out of bed, in fact. It *smells* great. Got any more?"

"No problem." She entered a code into the processor. "It does smell good, doesn't it?"

"Robots just don't understand decent food. I can't blame them, exactly, but—frost! Just imagine what we're missing! The first thing I want to do when we get to a real city is eat some good food for a change. A hot Kobe steak, say, with Magellanic frettage on the side and a bowl of ice cold—"

"That's it, Derec! The smell!" She spun around suddenly, with an excited smile. "Don't you get it?"

"What?"

"We should bring our hungry humans to us. Use the exhaust

fan to send out different food smells. We figure they're starving, right? We couldn't find them by chasing around, and now we have the robots doing that kind of search for us, anyway. In fact, I've been sending food smells outside all morning. It ought to work better, though, if we do it systematically."

"Couldn't hurt," he said cautiously. "Well—yeah! That could work! In fact, I can do something to help it along right now." He stuffed the rest of the piece of bacon into his mouth and sat down at the console. "The aromas alone won't go too far before they dissipate, but I'll enter this into the computer. It can alert robots to the fact that these smells represent substances edible to humans. So if our visitors ask, they'll be directed this way."

"I'll try to get more organized with this," she said. "I'll work up a rotation of dishes—protein, carbohydrates, and so on. After all, we don't know exactly what's most likely to get their attention."

"If they're really starving, they aren't going to be particular, but I'll leave that to you. Let's get to work."

Ariel had the most to do this time. She coded for various dishes and set them under the fan until they cooled. By the time one dish had stopped giving off its aroma, two more were ready. She put one of them under the fan, or even both, then reheated the preceding one. When each dish had dried out to no more than a shapeless, unrecognizable, desiccated blob, she scraped the remains into the recycler and punched the code for something else.

At one point, he requested more bacon, which interrupted her sequence for a short time. He took a break to work on the fan, and managed to squeeze a little more power out of it, but not much. They were still relying a great deal on chance and the help of the robots, who could direct their quarry to them.

Derec devoted the rest of his time to streamlining the central computer some more, or at least doing what he could. He had no more ideas left for locating alternate food sources, even now that he was fresh, so they were gambling entirely on her plan. As the day wore on, however, he began to feel a new kind of tension. He was restless, anxious to take some kind of action, but there was none to take. This plan simply called for waiting patiently until the bait worked.

"Most of this stuff really stinks," said Ariel. She left a new dish under the exhaust fan and started to wash her hands. "That bacon is the only one that really came out. I'm going to take a break and sit down."

"You're supposed to make the odors enticing," Derec said impishly. "We want to bring them in, not make them sick."

"Frost, Derec! You want to try it?" She demanded. "You try to figure out those stupid codes. Or stand here and inhale the fumes on some of these dishes that don't come out."

"Hey, take it easy. That was a joke."

"Some joke, smart guy. I don't see you helping us any."

"Oh, yeah? I suppose you could have done all the computer work I have since we've been together?" He turned from the screen to look at her.

"I didn't say that, and you know it."

"Maybe I'm not so sure. Maybe you do think I'm just along for the ride, now. Or don't you want me to streamline the computer anymore, like you were asking me before?"

"You're just pouting because I thought of the First Law point yesterday and the idea of sending out cooking smells today, that's all." She pulled her chair up facing her and sat down in it backwards, straddling the seat. "Admit it."

"It's not that simple. You told me you were out looking for adventure, remember? Wasn't that one of the reasons you left home?"

"One of them," she said icily.

"And you didn't get the kind of fun adventure you were thinking of, did you? Even getting away from Rockliffe Station the way we did was more glamorous than this. Going one-on-one with these robots all the time is more of a chore than an adventure."

"I'm also sick—remember?" she said quietly.

Derec broke eye contact, stung with embarrassment. Last night, in a moment of caring, they had carefully avoided the word. Now he'd let his temper ruin that.

"This computer work is getting to me," he said, also speaking softly. "I, uh, just can't seem to get as much done as I want."

"That's how I feel. There's too much work to do and nothing ever seems to help."

"It's the waiting, isn't it?"

"Yeah, partly. Just waiting here all day for someone to show up. And we don't know if they're within kilometers of here. They could be anywhere on the planet." She folded her arms across the back of the chair and leaned her chin down on them.

"We could take turns getting out. You know, just go for a walk. The city is pretty big; we haven't seen large parts of it, even now. You know, if we didn't have to work so hard at getting out of here, this would be an interesting place."

"I think I could use a walk. If you'll take the first shift here, maybe I'll get away from that processor for a while." She got off the chair with some effort. "What do you say?"

"Fair enough. While you're out, see how far away you can smell anything, okay?"

"Okay." She grinned over her shoulder in the doorway. "If it really does stink out there, I'll let you know."

Jeff did not get tired, but he did get sleepy. He didn't know enough physiology to explain that, but he assumed that having a human brain meant that he still required sleep. The problem, as night fell, was finding a place where he could sleep without interruption.

The city remained active at night, but safety was not the problem. In a city of robots, he had no fear of crime, so anyplace where he would not be awakened would be acceptable. However, he expected that the sight of him, as a robot, remaining motionless for a protracted period, might attract unwanted attention. He certainly didn't want a robot or two carrying him off bodily to a repair station because he had gone inert.

Jeff learned more about his robot eyes as he considered this problem. At first, as the sun went down and night came on, they opened in much the same degree as his human eyes had. They adjusted slowly and not really very much. Robot City had outdoor lighting, but it was not as bright as that of the cities on Aurora he had visited. The reason became obvious when night had fallen completely.

He was walking along the edge of a tiled plaza, hoping to

find a secluded spot where he could simply stop—reclining was not necessary—and go to sleep in private. As he peered into the darkness beyond the far edge of the plaza, the entire area suddenly grew much larger, practically flying at him. He straightened in surprise, then laughed at himself. His new eyes had a zoom capability that he had somehow triggered accidentally.

In order to test it, he stood where he was and tried to get his eyes to do something else. After looking at objects at several different distances, he found that if he focused on something as close as his own feet, his vision returned to normal and stayed that way. The zoom effect was triggered when he tried to focus for more than a few seconds on a distant object. If he just looked into the distance without trying to focus on detail, his vision remained normal.

More important at the moment, however, was his discovery of night vision. As he had experimented with his focal lengths, he had not noticed that the tile of the plaza, his robotic feet, and a low, decorative wall on the far edge of the plaza had all gradually become clearer. Now, as he looked around, he realized that he could see with a stunning clarity.

This, too, had happened automatically, like the narrowing and widening of human pupils. Only in this case, some other sensitivity was also built in. He didn't know what that sensitivity was, but he appreciated it. The objects around him were sharply outlined, illuminated by the city lighting that was sufficient when he used his new, robotic night vision. The only hint of darkness was in the distance, outside the range of the nearest lights.

His new vision sped up his search considerably. With a combination of night vision and zoom, he quickly eliminated the plaza area as a sleeping spot. He also realized that the robots would be able to see him with a similar ease, so finding a place to sleep would not depend on darkness. With that in mind, he began walking through areas that had unusually shaped architecture.

"All right," he said to himself. "I used to hide as a kid. This is basically the same thing. This ought to be easier than that, since I don't think anybody is really searching for me." He thought of the medical team, but decided that if they were looking for him, they were a long way off.

He had been hoping that the unusual architecture of some of the buildings might offer a small space where he could hide. Standing and lying flat were both equally unnecessary; he could actually squat down or double up in any fashion, without the usual danger of his limbs going to sleep, or needing to move to get more comfortable while he was sleeping.

The architecture did not help him, however. The more distinctive designs involved geometric shapes that had no small spaces in which he could crouch, and the simpler buildings were usually made up of modular rectangles of various proportions.

The other way to hide was in plain sight. He would have to look occupied, even while he was motionless in sleep. The tunnel system would provide that chance.

He went down into the first tunnel stop he found. The worst result he could think of was that he might not be able to stop at the same place he got on, but since he didn't know his way around the city anyway, that hardly mattered. He would be equally lost anywhere.

He stepped into a platform booth and looked in mystification at the controls. The best he could do was mark this particular stop. When he woke up, he could try to make it bring him back here. If that didn't work, he would stop anywhere he could.

Once the booth was on its way, he stood erect in a position that seemed casual enough and relaxed. At first, the noise of air rushing past the booth kept him awake, but then he remembered that he could control his hearing now, as well. He lowered his aural sensitivity, though he did not shut it off, and as he became fully relaxed, he felt himself to be the construct of two distinct parts. Earlier, he had felt integrated as a cyborg. Now he really felt himself to be a human brain housed in a motionless, manufactured unit that was just minimally active in order to keep his brain alive. It was a protective shell, apart from his own personal being in a way that his biological body never had been. In a few moments he was asleep, still standing up in the platform booth as it rushed through the tunnel system of Robot City.

Jeff woke up in nearly total disorientation. Ahead of him, a robot was standing in a transparent booth, speeding along a track down a mysterious tunnel. He looked around in alarm, and then suddenly his new life came back to him. Yes, his arms were still blue and robotic. He was still in this strange, manufactured body.

He was still all alone.

His ploy had worked, at least; none of the robots had bothered him while he slept.

He sensed vaguely that he had been dreaming, but he had no memory of the details. Nor did he think they had been pleasant.

He did figure out how to get the booth to carry him back to the same tunnel stop where he had entered. That accomplished, he rode up the ramp to daylight and looked around. He was satisfied that his one basic need, a place to sleep, had been arranged. Clothing was not necessary, and he knew that his robot body had an energy pack that was independent of ordinary food. He wasn't sure how it was able to keep his brain alive, but since it was working, he wasn't going to worry about it, either.

"Well, Jeffrey," he said aloud to himself. "It's time to start this new life of yours in earnest. Let's go see what we can see."

He stepped onto the slow lane of the nearest slidewalk and rode, gazing up at all the majestic, sweeping shapes of the city's most striking structures. The city was busier now than it had been the night before; he decided that perhaps the robots had scheduled indoor work for the night hours. His night vision had been very good, but it could not make up for a lack of sunlight.

He rode the slidewalk for a long time. Patience was not a problem, as the city both fascinated and worried him. Without a pressing schedule, or any physical needs to satisfy, he had nothing else to do. Every so often, he stepped off carefully onto an intersecting slidewalk and kept going. He still couldn't tell his way around, but, little by little, he began to recognize certain landmarks.

Even now, he looked about carefully everywhere. The medical team probably still wanted him, and any robot that suspected he was not susceptible to the Laws would be horrified by the idea. They wouldn't get him, though—not if he was careful.

Then, as the slidewalk carried him underneath some sort of transparent chute, a breeze came wafting to him from a new direction.

Jeff instinctively turned his head and inhaled—and became aware, for the first time, that he normally did not breathe in the usual human manner. Obviously, his brain needed oxygen, but the rest of his body did not require it. As he had with other questions about his new physiology, he dropped the question of how his body was taking in oxygen and supplying it to his brain; the fact of his continued existence proved that some process was working. He guessed that he could inhale largely for the purpose he was using now: to use a sense of smell.

"Magellanic frettage," he said quietly to himself, recognizing the aroma. He didn't want to be overheard, but the impulse to talk out loud was getting stronger. "Frettage in a kind of tangy sauce, I'd say. It smells great—I haven't had any of that in a long time. Let's go see."

He stepped off the slidewalk, caught his balance, and started walking in the direction of the scent. His body didn't need food, apparently, but the desire to taste enjoyable dishes was still with him. A number of his favorite dishes came to him: Magellanic frettage, Kobe steak, jiauzi, fresh strawberries. He wasn't sure if he could eat even if he wanted to, though he supposed not. Still, he could certainly enjoy smelling the stuff.

He was also hoping to find human companionship. "I wouldn't get my hopes up, Jeffrey ol' boy. You can't trust 'em with the truth, anyhow."

Traffic was moderately heavy here, but most of it was just function robots, which were no threat to him as they went about their business, unobservant and incurious. A few humanoid robots appeared from time to time, but none showed any interest in him. One robot, however, seemed to stay near Jeff, turning the same corners and walking in the same direction.

Jeff dropped back gradually, keeping a suspicious eye on this one robot. He did not appear to have noticed Jeff, but he had another odd quality. This robot was pushing a small, two-wheeled cart in front of him.

The cart, which had four solid gray sides but no lid, was weirdly primitive for this city of robots who could transplant a human brain, raise dynamic, glittering edifices, and guide what looked like a fully functioning society without human help. Lacking even its own power source, the cart was a throwback to ancient times.

Yet here it was.

• • •

Derec had continued to code some of Ariel's better dishes and place them under the fan, though the constant moving from the console to the processor and back prevented him from concentrating on streamlining the recalcitrant computer. He finally decided to take a real break from the computer and follow Ariel's lead with the chemical processor. At the very least, he might help improve the food they had to eat. Since the better codes had all been preserved, his failures wouldn't cost them anything, and success might make their existence here much more tolerable.

The Supervisor robots had arranged for them to be given a large supply of basic nutritional requirements in chemical form. These had been augmented by a harvest of edible plants out in the reservoir area. To produce an edible dish, various ingredients were mixed with water in the processor itself, and heated, according to the codes.

He started by trying to make the nutrition bars more tasty. First he got too much vanilla flavoring, though the result was definitely strong in flavor. When he attempted to add a hint of banana, he got something similar to a muddy-tasting Auroran root vegetable. It wasn't exactly good, but it certainly was different. He erased the code for that one, though he stuck the dish under the fan. Maybe his quarry liked Auroran root vegetables.

Ariel's bacon was nearly perfect, so he didn't mess with that. His first attempt at Magellanic frettage had come out more like over-boiled tyricus leaves in blue cheese, so he had recycled that one without even exhausting the aroma. Another attempt at that had been more successful, and the aroma was being fanned outside right now. He was trying to create a banana pudding when Ariel came back in.

"Yuck!" She winced and stuck out her tongue. "And I thought my stuff stunk. Frost, Derec, what did you kill in here?"

He laughed. "You're smelling my first batch of Magellanic frettage. The second one is better, and this new dish should also work. Banana pudding should be easy, don't you think?"

"If we don't die from the tyricus fumes first. Did my stuff smell this bad? If it did, I owe you an apology."

"No, not really. Could you smell anything outside?"

"Oh, yes. Basically, we're in pretty good shape. The configuration of the surrounding buildings has created a pretty constant horizontal wind, going from the fan, let's see, that way." She jerked her thumb. "The robot traffic is fairly heavy in that direction, so they can all help direct our people here. Now we just have to hope they get close enough to ask."

"The other way, though, nobody will smell anything."

"True, but the robots are circulating on their normal activities. They'll be spreading out all over the place."

"Okay. I hope this works. We've done just about everything."

She nodded. "If you want to take a turn stretching your legs, I'll take over here."

"Thanks. I think that pudding needs more water."

Derec strode outside with a spring in his step, glad to be in the open for a change. In the distance, however, the great shining dome of the Key Center seemed to taunt him. He refused to have his mood dampened, and turned away from it to start walking.

More out of curiosity than necessity, he located the breeze that she had mentioned. The banana pudding smelled pretty good, though he supposed starving people might prefer something more solid and nutritious. He stepped onto a slidewalk, but kept walking in a large rectangle around the general area. Actually spotting their human visitors didn't seem as unlikely as it once had, even if that was only a new optimism. As he came downwind of the breeze from the fan again, he was pleasantly surprised to recognize the scent of a decent dish of Magellanic frettage carried along by it. Perhaps her extra practice with the processor was paying off. Now that he had loosened up a little, he decided that he might as well head back. Waiting was still waiting, whether he sat inside or marched aimlessly around town.

When he arrived, Ariel was leaning in the doorway. She raised her eyebrows in surprise when she saw him.

"What are you doing back so soon? I thought the whole idea was for us to take turns in getting away for a bit."

"I did get away. Now I'm back."

"Frost, Derec. If I'd known that was all you were going to do, I would have stayed out longer myself. I came back early just for you."

"I wouldn't have cared if you'd stayed out longer. I didn't ask you to come back early."

"Well, do you mind if I go for another walk?"

"Of course not! Why are you making such a big deal of this?" As he waited for an answer, he stepped back from a humanoid robot walking toward them, assuming that the robot wanted to pass by.

"Oh, I don't know," she said irritably. "I guess this do-nothing phase just doesn't suit me very well."

The robot did not walk past them. He looked at Derec closely as, without stopping, he moved past him through the doorway.

"Hey," Derec said in surprise. "Can we help you? This is a private residence. Ours, that is."

The robot turned and looked back and forth between them.

"Identify yourself," Ariel commanded.

"Uh. . . ." The robot seemed uncertain, which was very rare in a robot.

"I gave you an *instruction*. Now identify yourself!"

"I, uh, I'm Tunnel Foreman, uh, 12."

"Say, wait a minute. That sounds familiar. Did I talk to you before? About the search?"

"Yes, you did."

"Well, why didn't you say so? If you came to report, Derec and I are the ones to report to. What have you learned?"

"I . . . haven't really learned anything."

"Then what are you doing here?" Derec asked. "Do you have a question?"

The robot hesitated, again looking back and forth between them as if in puzzlement.

"Something's wrong with him," said Ariel. "Get on the console and call a repair facility. He isn't acting right."

The robot started to leave.

"Stay here," Ariel ordered. When he didn't stop, she caught his arm. "I ordered you to stay put. What's wrong with you? Now freeze."

Derec had started inside, but when the robot yanked his arm free of Ariel, he stopped in shock. "Are you forgetting the Laws? You've been ordered to *freeze*."

The robot grabbed Ariel by the shoulders and flung her out of his way, slamming her against the wall. Derec launched himself between them, hoping to prevent the assault from continuing, even as disbelief flooded him. He saw the robot's arm swinging backhand toward him, but had no chance to react as the incredibly hard robot hand casually smacked him in the forehead and blackened his vision.

Derec felt himself fall backward into the wall and slide to the base of the doorway in a sitting position. He sat motionless for a moment, getting his breath back and gathering his wits. When he looked around, the robot was gone.

CHAPTER 12
TEAMWORK

Ariel scooted over to Derec with a look of concern. Even in his stunned condition, he appreciated it.

"You hurt bad, Derec?"

"No." His voice came out in a coarse mutter. "Got the breath knocked out of me, but that's all. How about you?"

"I'm all right. Thanks for getting in his way."

He grinned. "Any time, just so it isn't too often." He inhaled deeply a couple of times.

She took him under one arm and helped him to his feet. "Have you ever seen anything like that before?"

"Never. The positronic brains have always been totally reliable. That record is known everywhere." He dusted himself off. "I think the shock is worse than getting knocked down."

"This one's not reliable, that's for sure."

"Did you see where he went?" Derec looked down the street.

"No, but a couple of other robots went chasing after him. They must have been close enough to see what happened."

"I guess I heard a few footsteps. Let's go inside. I want to get on the console and find out if there's been any warning about a rogue robot."

She followed him inside. "The robots chasing him weren't

shouting or anything. I suppose they were all talking through their comlinks."

"I guess." He rubbed the back of his head where it had hit the wall, and winced. "I wonder what kind of insults robots exchange among themselves." He sat down at the computer and called up a variety of subjects—including warnings, city alerts, and suspected malfunctions. Nothing turned up.

"Maybe the malfunction just occurred," Ariel suggested. "We'll be the first ones to report."

"I'll do that. Let's see. . . . *Malfunctioning robot does not obey the Laws.* Since he actually attacked us, the rest of the robots will make searching for him a top priority. I imagine they'll even leave their regular jobs." He entered a description of the pertinent events.

"Doesn't it seem odd to you that he came here?"

"What do you mean?"

"We're the only people on the planet, that anyone can find. The others are lost. And this city is huge. Isn't it kind of strange that the one robot here who goes berserk just happens to wind up at the only apartment with humans in it?"

He paused for a moment at the keyboard. "I see what you mean. Of course, since the positronic failure involves the Laws, maybe he was drawn somehow to humans." He shrugged and continued on the console.

"They did know! Look at this—I got it when I entered the subject of *searches.*"

She leaned down close, reading over his shoulder. "Wait a minute. What kind of weird robot are they searching for?"

"I'm not sure he's exactly a robot at all. It says: *see Human Experimental Medical Team.* Let's see."

A moment later, he was reading in fascination. "He's human! Or at least, his brain is."

"His brain?"

"Look at this!" Derec pointed out the summary of the surgery on the computer's screen. "Unbelievable!"

"That's impossible," Ariel said, "transplanting a brain into a robot body."

"Everything's been impossible since we got here." Derec shook his head, as though to clear it. "We should be used to it by now."

"If you can ever get used to being surprised. What do we do now?"

"I'm trying to get the central computer to put me through to one of the robots on the medical team through their comlinks."

"Yes?" said a voice through the console.

"I am Derec, a human male. Please identify yourself."

"I am Human Medical Research 1, the Director of the Human Experimental Surgical Team."

"I have some information regarding a robot who doesn't obey the Laws of Robotics."

"Excellent. We have been conducting a pattern search from the perimeter of the city inward, with the help of many robots. Can you narrow the focus of search for us?"

"I'd like to see you and your team in person. Please come meet with Ariel and myself."

"We will do this. May I ask why you are delaying in providing me with helpful information?"

"This problem may be larger than it appears. The robot in question seriously disobeyed our instructions and physically attacked us. I think a major consultation is in order, don't you?"

"We will come at once." The robot's voice was suddenly formal and expressionless.

"Say—tell me one thing now. Has this guy's spacecraft been located? What kind of shape is it in?"

"It was destroyed on impact. What is your location?"

Disappointment struck Derec like a physical blow, but he gave them the information. Then he began pacing restlessly, trying to keep his spirits up. "At least the medical robot can tell us if he was traveling with the other two we've been looking for. It isn't over yet. We've made some kind of progress, believe it or not. It's about time." He slapped a fist into his other palm. "We still just might learn something we can use."

"You think this guy is one of the humans we're looking for?" Ariel, too, was crestfallen.

"I think so. Remember the third visitor, who just vanished after a certain point? This must be the one. I figure the reports of him stopped because he was in a robot body."

"I was hoping he had arrived on another ship. It would give us an extra chance." Disappointment was evident on her face.

The medical team arrived shortly. Derec told the three robots what had transpired and then asked for the relevant information they possessed. They briefed him on what they had told Jeff.

"So it's not a failure of the positronic brain," Research 1 finished. "However, we have consulted among ourselves and have concluded that we must enter a repair facility to have our brains removed and destroyed."

"What?" Derec cried. "You can't do that. We need your help."

"We created a situation in which a robot body violated the First Law by attacking humans. This is a violation of the First Law on our part. We would have reported immediately after the transplant surgery if we had understood where it would lead."

Derec looked at the two robot surgeons, who nodded in agreement. The three of them were standing together in a line, as though prepared for law-enforcement questioning. Maybe that was what they expected from a human, after violating the First Law.

"But you didn't attack anybody," said Ariel. "You were one step away from the situation. You can't take responsibility for what he—you said his name was Jeff?—decided to do."

"Besides, he didn't hurt us," said Derec. "It just surprised us. Well—totally shocked us, actually."

Surgeon 2 shook its head. "The extent of the harm is not a factor, since the Laws do not make allowances for degree. Nor is our ignorance of your presence a factor. The fact that we are one step removed from the incident is the only reason that we did not shut down upon learning of this violation of the First Law. If we had directly harmed a human, the trauma to our systems would have completely neutralized our functioning. However, this individual would not exist in the unusual form he does without our contribution. He is unique, and is our responsibility."

"Look at it this way," said Ariel anxiously. "We need help. If Jeff is still out there running around, he could conceivably do more harm to us. Doesn't the First Law require you to cooperate with us?"

"We have proven our judgment irresponsible," said Surgeon 1. "You cannot rely on us. Therefore, we should be destroyed."

"You haven't violated the Laws any other time, have you?" Derec pointed out.

"No, but we have no other history of contact with humans," said Research 1. "In our initial contact with humans, we contributed to a violation—"

"Of the First Law, I know. You don't have to keep repeating it," said Derec. "But I shouldn't have phrased the question that way. You still haven't broken the Laws. Jeff did, sort of. Only, since he doesn't have a positronic brain, that doesn't really count."

"Our information about human behavior is apparently incomplete," said Research 1. "We did not understand the likelihood of Jeff's attack on you. In fact, the central computer did not even inform us of your presence. We felt his medical condition was such that the First Law required our attempting the transplant. However, one purpose of the First Law that I infer is to preserve humans from the greater strength of our robot bodies. So to us, Jeff in this case counts as a robot, despite his lacking a positronic brain. This judgment will not be imperative on his brain, of course."

"If the First Law required you to perform the transplant, how can you blame yourselves?" Ariel asked. "That seems like a real contradiction. One that I wouldn't expect from the logical mind of a robot."

"The logical contradiction has only become evident now," said Surgeon 1. "In the sequence of events as they unfolded, the First Law has made clear requirements of us, including our elimination."

Derec looked at them helplessly, unable to think of an argument against their destruction that they had not countered already.

"Postpone your trip to the repair center," Ariel suggested. "If you think it's required, you can do it later. Right now, we really need your help, like we said."

"That's right," said Derec quickly. "How about this? The First Law requires that you help us catch Jeff and, I don't know —stop him somehow. Then you can destroy yourselves."

The three robots hesitated long enough to reveal that this argument had carried some weight.

"Isn't it your responsibility to help clean up the mess?" Ariel added, with a triumphant smile. "The Second Law requires that you follow our orders to help. Since you have never directly violated any of the Laws, including the First, you're reliable enough for us."

"This is acceptable to me," said Research 1. "We shall retain the option of having our brains destroyed later, in any case."

"I find it acceptable, also," said Surgeon 1. "Unnecessary destruction of our brains would be an inefficient handling of material, energy, and experience. We should logically establish the necessity of this move beyond any doubt, with as much gathering of relevant evidence as possible."

"Whew," said Surgeon 2. The robot looked at Derec. "That is the human vernacular appropriate to the occasion, is it not?"

"Sure is." Derec laughed in relief. "Okay. That problem is solved. Next problem. We want information from this guy about getting off the planet. You just want to make sure he can't violate any of the Laws. What's our plan of action?"

"You will have to take the lead in direct confrontation," said Research 1. "Any plans will have to take this into account."

"What do you mean?" Ariel asked.

"Since we know that Jeff has a human brain," said Surgeon 1, "we are subject to the Laws when dealing with him. We could not disobey his instructions, for instance, if he told us to leave him alone. Or worse, to forget that he exists at all."

"Hold it," said Ariel, holding up a hand. "You're upset about his breaking the laws because he's a robot, but now you say you have to obey the Laws where he's concerned because he's human. Aren't you contradicting yourselves?"

"No," said Research 1. "In regard to the Laws, he is both human and robot. We cannot deny him the combination of traits that we ourselves gave him. All the advantages are therefore his. This makes him very powerful."

"What about that pattern search you told me you started?" Derec asked. "How were you going to catch him when you located him?"

"Our only hope was to talk him into cooperating. We could not use violence in contradiction to the Laws. However, he will at some point be in danger to his health. At that point, of course, we would be able to force our aid on him."

"What kind of danger?" asked Ariel. "He's got a robot body."

"His robot body is powered by a standard energy system," said Surgeon 2. "However, his organic brain requires nutrition and oxygen. We installed a container of vital nutrients and synthetic hormones in the lower portion of his head, and part of his neck, and a routing system to his brain. These chemicals are delivered to his brain through its existing circulatory system by synthetic blood. Oxygen is also delivered this way, supplied by the breaths he will take from time to time."

"Understood so far," said Derec. "Go on."

"He can't eat in the normal human sense. So his nutrient pack must be refilled at certain intervals. He does not know this."

"He doesn't? Why didn't you tell him?" Ariel demanded.

"He ran away before we started briefing him. We wanted to test him first. We did not know he would leave before we could inform him of this." Surgeon 2 looked at Research 1. "Since our tests were not complete, we do not know precisely how successful the transplant has been."

"That is true," said Research 1. "There are considerable unknowns regarding his health. That is why an interpretation of the First Law allows us to help you find him."

"I've been thinking about a question Ariel asked me a while ago," said Derec. "Do you think Jeff came here, to our residence, for a reason? Or was it just a random visit?"

"The odds against a human, such as he is, making a random visit to the only human dwelling in the city are too high to take seriously," said Surgeon 2.

"Your use of human food smells to attract fellow humans here may have influenced him," said Research 1. "He is not yet in need of nutrition. However, previous habits and the stimulation of the pleasure center in his brain by the food aromas may have created a desire to experience the smell and taste of human food."

"I don't suppose it would work a second time," said Ariel. "Getting away seemed awfully important to him. If he can't eat anyway, he wouldn't really need to come back here."

"A logical assumption," said Research 1.

"All right, hold it," said Derec. "I'd like to go at this in a straight line, if you don't mind. As I see it, we have three problems. In order to get ahold of this guy Jeff, we have to locate him and identify him and grab him. Is this pattern search of yours going to capture him? How does it work?"

"It employs the entire robot population of Robot City," said

Research 1. "However, they do not have to leave their duties. We have set up a net of testing around the perimeter of the city, moving inward, that goes from one robot to the next. No robot will work with any other or allow any other to pass, unless the other robot can demonstrate the use of his comlink. Since Jeff does not have this ability, he will eventually be identified."

"We could have built a radio system into his body," said Surgeon 1. "It seemed an unnecessary contradiction to his human identity, so we chose not to do so."

"Good thing," said Derec. "It sounds like your search could take a long time, though. If he's smart, and wants to escape notice, he can keep away from your search until the very last minute. And if he's lucky, he might sneak through the ring as it closes."

Surgeon 2 shook its head. Unlike most Avery robots, he seemed to like these gestures. "It is not a ring, but a solid circle. Even if he moves out into the previously tested area without being identified, he will still be challenged by every robot who sees him. The testing will not cease until we report that he has been detained."

Derec nodded in approval. "Not bad. I still say it will take a while, unless he gets careless."

"Agreed," said Research 1. "It could take an extended period of time, but it will identify him without fail. Chances of his capture will be maximized if we have one of you, the humans, on hand to detain him, however. Otherwise, the Second Law will allow him to order us away unless a First Law imperative instructs us to override his orders."

"What are we supposed to do?" Ariel turned her hands palm up and looked around at the three robots. "We can't order him around any more than you can. And he's stronger than you are."

The robots were silent.

"We'll worry about that later," Derec decided. "The first job is to get him identified. Maybe we can think of a way to short cut the search process."

"Perhaps so," said Research 1. "We are at your disposal."

"So to speak," added Surgeon 2.

CHAPTER 13
LIFE ON THE RUN

Jeff was on the run. He had shoved Derec and Ariel aside in a frenzied panic, aching to speak with fellow humans and yet terrified of being discovered—though he didn't know why that mattered. The robot pursuit, driven by their horror of an apparent robot violating the First Law, the fundamental rule of their existence, was much greater now than it had been before. It was a testimonial to the imperative of the First Law that now, as he ran, every humanoid robot in the area dropped its duties to give chase, informed silently of his transgression by the comlinks of two robots that had happened to witness his physical assault on the humans.

Even the function robots began to impede him as he ran down the street, apparently ordered by the robots already in pursuit. Without positronic brains, the function robots could not make any advanced judgments of their own, but they could follow instructions. Little sweepers and couriers began zigzagging in front of him; giant construction equipment, intelligent enough not to require drivers, blocked his path down other streets. Behind him, all manner of weirdly shaped devices had joined the growing number of humanoid robots chasing him down the street.

"Come on, Jeffrey; come on, Jeffrey," he thought to himself as he ran, the rhythm of the phrase keeping time with his beating footsteps. He was even starting to breathe again, perhaps because the stress had caused a greater need for oxygen in his brain, even though his physical activity would not have caused that need. What a time to think about his physiology, he sneered at himself.

Ahead of him, more robots of all kinds were shifting to cut off his escape. They almost had him—no! On the right, an open tunnel stop invited him. He angled for it on a collision course with a large, block-shaped function robot with a variety of flexible tentacles ending in tools. The function robot rolled to a stop, filling the entrance to the tunnel. Jeff grimaced—at least on the inside — and reflexively clenched his steel jaw as he collided with it.

Jeff bounced away, but caught at one of the extended tentacles to maintain his footing. The impact had shoved the function robot back just enough for him to slide past one of its corners and run down the ramp. He nearly stumbled as the ramp started to move, and he ran, tripping on his toes, into the nearest booth. This time he knew how to work the controls, and took off quickly into the dim light of the tunnel.

He looked back once, and saw the crowd of humanoid robots pouring down the ramp and entering platform booths. The function robots had been eliminated from the chase, since the booths were designed for intelligent, humanoid passengers. He faced forward again, now trying to blend with the other robots riding in booths.

He shifted to one of the mid-speed lanes and looked nonchalant. In a way, he was new at losing himself in the crowd, and yet, after being highly visible all his life, this was ridiculously easy. Some of the robots in pursuit came alongside, and others passed him, but they could not distinguish between him and the others. He had no way of knowing if they were trying to reach him through their comlinks or not, but if so, they didn't seem to know who was answering and who was not. All the robots within sight were standing in roughly the same position, confined in booths the same way.

When a couple of robots rode into the siding at the next tunnel stop, some of the pursuing robots followed them. Jeff realized then that the longer he remained riding the platform, the thinner the pursuit would become. So he stayed where he was, occasionally changing lanes as though he were traveling in a deliberate manner to a specific destination.

It worked.

He smiled to himself as he rode. Three times, now, he had escaped robots that were chasing him. Nor had he outmuscled them—if he could use that term for robot arms. He had had to outsmart them, in the end, since they were physically as strong as he was. And if they ever really got hold of him, he would claim his rights as a human to consideration under the Laws of Robotics.

They were no match for him.

Only other humans had the same ultimate power over the robots that he did, based on the Laws . . . but, of course, they would be much weaker physically. He realized, for the first time, that he was actually the single most powerful individual on the entire planet. If he was careful, he could do anything here that he wanted.

Of course, he had no idea of how the city was governed. Perhaps the robots had some kind of city council or something. It didn't matter, since they would have to obey him if he decided to reveal himself and give them orders. He had to make sure they couldn't catch him, though.

He shook his head slightly, trying to remember why he didn't want to be caught. Nor could he figure out why he was afraid of the robots, if they had to obey his orders. It didn't make sense, but that was how he felt.

Maybe those two humans could join him. Of course, they would have to undergo the same transplant surgery that he had. Then all three of them would be virtually invincible, not only against the robots, but against any other humans who might come to this planet. They might not like the idea, but it could be done without their agreement. After all, he hadn't had any chance to discuss the matter, either.

"Well, well, well," he said aloud. "A conspiracy. A takeover. So I do have something to accomplish here, after all."

He had been carefully watching the robots traveling around him, and knew that the ones pursuing him had all left the tunnel system by now. To increase his distance from them, he rode a little longer, then stopped at a siding chosen at random. Now that he was out of their sight, he didn't think they could pick him out again.

Once back on the surface, he got on the slidewalk to ride until he got his bearings. With safety as close as any tunnel stop, he was free to roam. At the same time, he wanted to communicate with his human colleagues if he could do so without having robots jump all over him.

When he had picked out a few landmarks, principally a huge, shining dome and a strange, many-sided pyramid, he worked his way back toward the human residence. All the while, he looked about carefully for any sign that robots were conducting a search. He didn't see any evidence of a continuing search in the area, but he had to be careful.

He was in the neighborhood, now, but still kept riding the slidewalk around in a series of jagged circuits, looking for a trap. His human colleagues, as he thought of them, were not in sight. The robot traffic here was light, and seemed to be safe enough.

He started to look in the other direction, when a familiar shape caught his eye. When he glanced back, he saw that same robot pushing the wheeled handcart again. On impulse, he leaped off the slidewalk and walked briskly up behind the robot.

"Are you following me?" he demanded.

The robot stopped and turned around. "Are you addressing me?"

"Yes. Identify yourself."

"I am Alpha."

Jeff hesitated. "Alpha? That's all?"

"Yes."

"That doesn't sound like the other names in this place. Why are you different?"

"I am not a native construct of this planet. Please identify yourself."

"I'm Jeff. If you're a stranger here, then we have something in common. I thought you were following me around."

"Not at all. Our proximity must be a coincidence. However, you may be able to aid me."

"Are you willing to join up with me? The two of us, we don't have any particular place in this society. I'm . . . gathering friends, you might say. Followers."

"I have no objection to this."

"Fair enough. What can I do for you?"

Alpha pulled a cloth from the wheeled cart. A small, furry creature lay inside, its eyes closed and its pointed ears limp and flat. Clumps of brown and gold fur had been falling out, revealing leathery skin under it. "This is an intelligent non-human named Wolruf. She is starving. I came to this planet with her. However, food for her has been scarce. Can you find some?"

"I'm not sure," said Jeff, looking at the little alien doubtfully. She had a caninoid body. "You ask anybody else? Any of these robots who live here?"

"Yes. However, since I have determined that she is non-human, the Laws do not apply and they are not required to help save her. The robots I have questioned here do not know where to find food for her, and have no greater ability to locate any than I. So the responsibility remains mine."

"I think you've met up with the right pers—individual."

"Can you help? We explored near a lake that I believe to be a reservoir and found a few plants that helped keep her alive, but that is all. I surmise that she requires a concentration of proteins they did not provide."

"It so happens that I smelled some food—human food, that is—in this very neighborhood. In a town like this, it must have been prepared in some kind of autogalley, like they have on shipboard. That would mean it could be altered to prepare other kinds of chemical food."

"I smelled it also," said Alpha. "This is what brought me to this area. However, the winds come and go. I lost the scent for a short time, and when I recovered it, an altercation of some kind was taking place among robots. Since I have chosen to make Wolruf's safety a priority, I was forced to leave the immediate vicinity."

"I see." Jeff chose not offer any additional information about that particular altercation.

"And since that time, I have not been able to locate any odors of the same type."

"Ah. Well." Jeff paused, not sure how to proceed. He wanted to get this little doggie-thing some food, to win over his new friend. On the other hand, he did not want to be identified again. To stall for time, and to satisfy his curiosity, he nodded at the cart. "Where'd you get that contraption?"

"I constructed it from scrap materials on the edge of the city, where new urbanization is taking place."

"Very clever. Well. Hmm." This little cart impressed him. It was so simple. A robot who could do this kind of thing on his own resources, and who had no ties to Robot City, was definitely an asset.

Jeff decided that he could not risk returning to the human residence. Nor did he want to turn over his new friend to other humans, who could give orders contradictory to his own, and perhaps even turn Alpha against him. He couldn't trust anybody. Yet he had to find a solution.

Another humanoid robot was walking toward them. Jeff chose, on the spot, to take a different kind of risk, one that would allow him to make a run for cover if necesssary.

"Halt and identify yourself," he said to the approaching robot.

"For what purpose?" The robot halted, however.

"I have instructions for you."

"I am Architectural Foreman 112. Identify yourself."

"My name is Jeff." He sighed, and then fixed his gaze carefully on Architectural Foreman 112. "I am human."

Beside him, Alpha looked up with new attention.

"Perhaps you are malfunctioning. Your comlink might be more efficient. I thought you said that you are human," said Foreman 112.

"I am. My human brain was surgically transplanted into a robot body. However, the Laws of Robotics apply to me as a human. You must obey my instructions. Understand?"

Foreman 112 studied him. "I understand. I have just contacted the central computer, and have been informed that this transplant took place into a body of your type and that you have been reported in this neighborhood very recently."

"Good. Now—"

"You are also the object of a search. The Human Experimental Medical Team urgently requests your presence and cooperation."

"Now, you just forget about that. They don't have any right

to capture me. I haven't done anything wrong." He eyed the robot suspiciously. "Did you tell them where I am?"

"I have reported your location here at the request of the central computer."

"Shut up and listen to my orders! Now, look inside this thing. This cart holds a little—creature that is dying of starvation. Its friend here is named Alpha. I'm instructing you to build, or arrange the building, of an autogalley that can feed this, this—"

"Her name is Wolruf," Alpha repeated. "She is an intelligent non-human."

"Yeah, right."

Foreman 112 looked at Wolruf. "Would the location of an existing chemical processor be acceptable? One is in storage. This would provide nutrition much faster."

"That one's okay," Jeff said carefully. "But only that one. Understand? Nobody else's. Got it?"

"It is the only one I have knowledge of," said Architectural Foreman 112. "It should suffice in this emergency."

"Good. Okay. You take Alpha and Wolruf to wherever it is. Alpha, can you explain what kind of food she needs?"

"Yes."

"Okay. Uh—I have to get out of here at the moment, since this traitor has reported my location." He glared at Architectural Foreman 112. "I want to talk to you again, Alpha, but. . . ." He couldn't tell Alpha where to meet him in front of this other robot, who would report him again. "Never mind where. I'll worry about that later. I'll give you this order: if I try to meet with you in secret someplace, you cooperate. Got it?"

"Yes," said Alpha.

"All right. On your way, you two."

Jeff watched them just long enough to be satisfied that they were leaving together. He felt a sense of accomplishment on several grounds: Alpha now owed him a favor, and he had convinced Architectural Foreman 112 that he was a human for whom the Laws applied. If he proceeded carefully, he really might take over Robot City.

"Well, well, Jeffrey. So far, so good. Maybe your life has a purpose after all, know what I mean?"

The last building block he needed in order to create a powerful following was the support of the other humans. He didn't dare visit them in person until he found out how they felt about him, but he could safely contact them from a distance. First, however, he had to get away from here.

"All right, Jeffrey. Back into the labyrinth again. They'll never find you in your second home."

As before, he used the tunnel system to shake the chase. This time he departed before any pursuit came into view. The tunnel system, unless it was shut down completely, remained the perfect escape. The individual booths kept him isolated and the tunnels had so many stops and branches that his chance of losing himself down there was very good. After another long ride, he came up again at a random spot and went to the edge of the nearest slidewalk.

As he waited for a humanoid robot to ride the slidewalk his way, he seriously considered the possibility that the robots running the city might actually shut down his tunnel system. It wouldn't break the Laws. This crazy city might have other places he could sleep in peace, and it almost certainly would offer other ways of escaping pursuit. He just hadn't had time to find out what they were yet.

"Hey, where is everybody? What's going on?"

He glanced around, puzzled. Everywhere else in the city, humanoid robots had been more or less everywhere. He could see a few in the distance now, but none were coming past him.

"Ho, ho, Jeffrey ol' boy. Time to get smart, maybe, eh? Something isn't quite normal. No sense just standing out here to frost. Let's just take a little trip, visit the tunnel again, see the sights."

Now leery of a trap, he turned and fled back down the tunnel stop. Moments later, he was shooting through the underground system again in one of the booths, looking at the robots in other booths all around him. What if they were part of the trap? Maybe he was being escorted, herded, to wherever they wanted him to go.

"Calmly, calmly," he said aloud in the booth. "Maybe they don't know anything for sure. Maybe they're trying to smoke you out. Look like everybody else, remember?" He started giggling to himself. "That's it. Stay calm and look like all the others."

He did so, secretly looking over the other robots traveling in the tunnels. None of them seemed to pay any attention to him.

"Shaken the pursuit again, have you?" he said out loud. "Very good, very good. This will work. This project will work. Now, let's get on with it."

Still, some time passed before he decided that he could safely return to the surface again. Then he picked another stop at random and reemerged into the sunlight. Now he was once more in an area of the city with a fair amount of humanoid traffic on the slidewalks, as he had been used to seeing. In the distance, the tall pyramid glinted in the sunlight, giving him a reference point.

He flagged down the first humanoid robot who came riding by, and identified himself as human. Like the last robot he had approached this way, Energy Pack Maintenance Foreman 3928 verified his claim with the central computer.

"I am satisfied that you are Jeffrey Leong, a human," said E Pack Foreman 3928.

"Good. Then under the Second Law, you know—"

"As a positronic robot, I am familiar with the Laws of Robotics."

"All right!" Jeff shouted. "Then get this! Don't ever interrupt me again! You understand, you slag heap?"

"I understand," the robot said blandly.

"You'd better. Come to think of it, that moniker of yours is too long. From now on, you answer to Can Head. Got it?"

"Yes."

"What's your name?"

"My name is Energy Pack Maintenance Foreman 3928. I will also answer to Can Head."

"Well . . . good enough, I guess." Jeff laughed. "Now listen to this. I want to contact the two humans living here in Robot City. I've met them, and I think they're the only ones here. You use your comlink or whatever it is to get ahold of them. That's an order," he added, leaning close and staring into Can Head's eyeslit.

"I have just checked with the central computer. I can go through it to a computer console in their dwelling. However, I lack the capacity to transmit your voice directly."

"Yeah? You aren't lying to me, are you, Can Head?"

"I lack that capacity, as well."

"Hmm—maybe. You should. Unless things aren't as they seem around here. Nothing in this town is right, if you ask me. Only, how can I trust you to pass on what I say? What if you play around a little with the content? Or don't report what they say back to me just like they say it? What about that?"

"I lack the capacity for deceit."

"What do you need to transmit my voice directly? A microphone and some other equipment, I guess, huh?"

"Yes."

"Let's go find some. You get it and arrange for me to contact them directly. Get going."

CHAPTER 14
THE TRANSPLANT

Ariel sat at the console, trying to think up other subjects that might tell her something about Jeff or his whereabouts. Derec was out with the medical team, making plans to catch him. The search for Jeff had given Derec and Ariel a new focus for their attempt to get off the planet, and the fact that they had actually seen him made their chances seem more tangible. Her spirits were up again, even if Jeff's spacecraft had been destroyed on impact.

She had just left the console to take a break when a voice came through the speaker.

"Hello! Hey, you! Answer me."

She slid back into the seat, puzzled by the odd greeting. That wasn't the kind of courtesy one received from robots. "Identify," she answered cautiously.

"I don't have to identify unless I feel like it. This is the robot that knocked you two down. The Laws don't apply to me." He paused. "You know what I'm talking about?"

"Jeff," said Ariel excitedly. "Uh, hi. Where are you?"

Weird robot laughter buzzed through the speaker. "You can't fool me that easy. Say, how did you know my name? What's your name: You're pretty, as I recall."

"I'm Ariel." She wanted to keep him talking and see if she could persuade him into coming in. If not, maybe he would slip up and say something that would give away his location. "Can I help you? What are you calling about?"

"If you know my name, you must have talked to those robot doctors, huh? So you know how I got this way."

"Yes, and they told us you need to come in for your health. They didn't finish the tests, and you don't know how to take care of yourself yet. You left before they could explain." She eyed the keyboard, wondering if she could have the central computer contact the medical team while she kept Jeff in conversation.

"Oh, sure; I have to come in for my own good, right? Frost, I'm not that stupid."

"Jeff, what are you afraid of? They're robots. They can't do anything to harm you." She started tapping the keys carefully, not wanting to make any noise he might hear.

"Don't let them fool you, kid. If they're so helpful, why don't they transplant you? You'd like it this way. So would your friend. What's his name, anyhow?"

"His name is Derec. What do you mean, why don't they transplant me? They were trying to help you because you were injured in the crash when you landed. Why would I want to have my brain transplanted?" She continued on the keyboard.

"They helped me, all right. Don't you get it, Ariel? I like this. I'm better this way."

"Better? You mean you like having a robot body?" She stopped typing, shocked. "I thought you might be mad at them for doing this. You sound angry about something."

"Angry? Frost, what for? I'm the most powerful individual on this entire planet."

"What do you mean?" She completed entering the instruction for Derec and the medical team to return as fast as they could, and why. If they could intercept Jeff's broadcast and eavesdrop, they should attempt that in the meantime. Triangulating on his beam and trapping him would be best of all.

"What do I mean? Are you crazy? It's obvious! I'm stronger than you or any other human, and I'm free of the Laws. Completely free of them! I have every physical advantage of a robot and every privilege of being human. I can do anything I want. Anything! Don't you *understand?*" He was screaming now.

She hesitated, surprised by the sound of a robot voice yelling at her in frustration. "I understand," she said calmly. "It's okay, Jeff. I understand."

"Do you?" He demanded suspiciously.

"Sure. It makes sense. You're unique. No one has ever lived the way you're living now. You're the very first. Uh, tell me what it's like. It must be interesting." Since she had no idea where Derec and the medical team were, she couldn't estimate their time of arrival. All she could do was keep talking.

"What it's like?" He sounded surprised. "Well . . . it's different. Very different. Everybody thinks I'm a robot, for one thing. You look like everybody else. No one knows who you are. Your body can do different things, too. For instance, you can see better and hear better and smell better. And you can sleep standing up."

She laughed. "What?"

"Forget it," he said brusquely. "Never mind that part. Forget I mentioned it."

"You like to sleep standing up?"

"I said forget it!" He shouted. "Besides, any robot can do that. Stop, I mean, in a fixed position. They don't sleep, of course. That's all I meant. They can all do that, can't they? Huh?"

"Yes, they can. Take it easy. It's okay." She hesitated, realizing that she certainly couldn't predict what would set him off on a tirade. "How old are you, Jeff?"

"Uh—eighteen. Sort of. In this life, I'm just a couple days old." He laughed, much too hard. Then he stopped abruptly. "Actually, I don't know how long I had this body before I woke up. I have no birthday any more, not in this body."

"Eighteen? Really? I guess I thought you'd be older. Were you in school? I mean, before you got here." She tried to sound as sympathetic as she could.

"I was on my way to college," he said quietly.

She sensed that this was a sore subject, and dropped it. "Where are you from, Jeff?"

"The planet Aurora."

"Really?" She said brightly. "I'm from Aurora, too, and I'm just a little younger than you are. In fact—" She hesitated, then decided to say it. "I'm Ariel Welsh."

"Ariel Welsh . . . really? The famous one?"

"Well . . ." The reminder stung. "I guess so. Juliana Welsh is my mother."

"So this is where you wound up! Wow. I'm really talking to you? You were in all the news and everything." Suddenly he sounded his age, and guileless.

Ariel said nothing.

"That does it," he said firmly. "You order those robots to transplant you. You're sick, right? Well, you won't be sick in a robot body. Unless the infection has reached your brain, too, of course. So you tell them, all right? Then after that, you can join me."

Ariel was reeling. If it could work, it might stop the spread of the disease. Her body could be frozen while a cure was found, and she could go on living as a robot. Why hadn't she thought of that?

"Hey! You there? Hey, Ariel!" He yelled.

Of course, she might have to stay on Robot City, in that case. Then again, as a robot, she would fit in a little better. No, much better. Nor would she feel that she was wasting her life here. The biological life expectancy of her body wouldn't start up again until it was thawed out, whenever that could be arranged. Her brain would age normally if it was functioning in a robot body, but maybe the disease would not affect her brain, or at least not as fast. She could encourage the medical team to work on a cure. The First Law would require that, wouldn't it?

"You still there?" Jeff demanded.

"Yes! Yes, I'm here. Don't go—I'm interested."

"You are?" He sounded surprised again, then he recovered. "Of course you are! I knew you would be. It's better this way. We can take over the city together. Now, how about Derec?"

"Huh? What about him?"

"The transplant, of course! Aren't you listening to me? What's wrong with you?"

"He doesn't have any reason to be transplanted."

"Of course he does! That's what I've been telling you! He can see better, hear better, and all that. He'll like it. And the three of us can take over the planet. The robots will have to obey us. Think of it—an entire planet at our disposal."

"I'm not sure he's going to see it that way." She added to herself that Derec's amnesia was in his mind. Transplanting his brain wouldn't take care of that problem.

"Of course he will. It's easy to understand. He'll get it."

"Why would we want to take over the planet?"

"So it would be ours, of course. What kind of question is that? We could run it."

"Actually, the robots run it pretty well, don't you think? Everything runs smoothly here."

"But it would be ours!"

"But what would we do with it? What would be different? The robots would still do all the work, just like they do now."

"It would be *ours!* Don't you understand? The entire planet would belong to us."

"Okay, Jeff, okay. But if nothing changes, those are just words. Ownership wouldn't mean much, would it? The robots obey us already, so that won't get any better."

"You'll see! If you get this transplant, you'll understand. Then you'll find out, just like I did."

Ariel started to answer, then realized that the static had stopped: he was gone. She let out a deep breath, and sagged back in the chair with the release of tension. At this point, she didn't mind having to wait a little while for the others to return. He had given her several things to think about.

Derec was breathless when he ran into the room, followed by his concerned but calm robot companions. "Is he still on the line? I want to talk to him."

"Too late," said Ariel. "I kept him on as long as I could, but I ran out of stuff to say."

"We overheard part of it, but not too much."

"He must have been using a very primitive radio set," said Surgeon 2. "The quality of our reception varied greatly as we traveled through the city on our return trip."

"Do you know where he is?" Derec asked.

"No. He was very suspicious, and, well, kind of strange." She looked at the robots. "Was he like that before?"

"Like what?" Research 1 asked.

"He sounded almost paranoid. And he kept going through mood swings. One minute he's laughing and the next minute he's totally enraged. Then he forgets it all and makes ordinary conversation." She shook her head. "It just wasn't normal."

"No," said Research 1. "He was not like that in the brief time he was awake with us."

"He was in a post-operative state at that time," said Surgeon 1. "He was surprised, and perhaps shocked. Nor was he conscious when we first found him. His behavior during the brief time he was awake with us may not have been representative of his personality."

"You mean he might always have been erratic and emotionally unstable?" Derec asked.

"Possibly," said Research 1. "Our data is too limited for a sound conclusion."

"I have another theory," said Ariel. "Do you think something is going wrong with him in some way?"

"Clarify, please," said Research 1.

"Well, he's been through a lot," she pointed out. "And at times he sounded normal and friendly. He was on his way to college somewhere. If he got accepted off-planet, outside Aurora, he was probably a good student."

"Agreed," said Derec. "You think the transplant has changed his personality, then."

They both turned to Research 1.

"How likely is it?" Ariel asked.

"This is possible. The odds cannot be calculated under the circumstances."

"Well—what do you think might have gone wrong?" She decided not to express the reason for her new interest in the transplant right now.

"Without precise medical data, I can offer two general possibilities. One is that the emotional shock of finding himself in a robot body has distressed him to the point of behavioral change. The second is that his brain is suffering from a chemical imbalance that has caused this problem. It might be nutritionally or hormonally based, or might indicate a flaw in our procedure or planning."

"Can you help him?" asked Ariel. "If we catch him, I mean. He doesn't seem too far gone yet."

"That will depend on the precise nature of the problem, of course," said Research 1.

"We may have a full solution to the larger problem of Jeff, however," said Surgeon 1. "With your cooperation, Derec."

"What? Mine?"

"We are capable of intricate surgical techniques," said Surgeon 1. "And we have a great deal of information of certain types regarding human physiology and medical care. However, we lack certain basic information regarding gross anatomy and some details of all kinds."

"I don't know anything like that," said Derec. "I don't think it's in the central computer, either."

"You don't need to," said Medical Research 1. "We need your body as a model."

Ariel stifled a laugh.

"How so?" Derec asked carefully. "What do you mean, as a model?"

"We need information regarding the complete physiology of a young human male, particularly regarding the arrangement of inner organs, in order to restore Jeff's body to a healthy condition. Yours can act as a kind of map."

"Pardon me for asking this," said Derec, "but exactly what do you need from me? In particular, uh. . . ."

"You will not be subjected to any risk," said Research 1. "After all, the First Law would not permit risk in your case, as it did in Jeff's. We have the ability to construct scanning systems that will tell us what we must know without surgical procedures or drugs."

Derec visibly relaxed. "Okay, sure. But we still have to get our hands on Jeff."

"Granted," said Research 1. "Nevertheless, we will arrange to have the systems constructed, since they do not currently exist. It will not take very long. The odds are very high in favor of Jeff's eventual apprehension, limited only by his unknown medical condition and the chance of injurious accident to his brain. Damage to the rest of him can, of course, be fully repaired."

"Brain damage would require a great deal of trauma," observed Surgeon 2. "His cranial protection was especially designed for him, as demanded by the First Law, and is highly effective."

"Good," said Derec. "We definitely need information from him, and the saner he is, the better. A crazy guy's answers aren't going to help us much."

"Enough about my conversation with him," said Ariel. "What about you? Did you get anything accomplished while you were out there? Or didn't you have enough time?"

"We rearranged the pattern of the ongoing search," said Research 1. "The closing doughnut has been speeded up, based on the First Law concern regarding Jeff's health. We have charged some additional robots inside the remaining hole here in the center of the city with the same behavior. This may locate him a little faster."

"I believe the colloquial phrase is, 'smoke him out'," said Surgeon 1. "Is that correct?"

"Yes." Ariel laughed.

"I told them that putting more pressure on Jeff might push him into a mental mistake," said Derec.

"I think so," said Ariel. "He's gotten very short-tempered."

"Maybe it's just as well that robots are out looking, if he's going to get violent." Derec turned to the robots. "Now we're just back to waiting, I guess, for the time being. We'll contact you immediately if we have a new development."

"Very well," said Research 1. "We shall return to our facility and prepare the scanning systems."

When they had left, Ariel got up so that Derec could have the console chair if he wanted it. Instead, he started into his room.

"Derec?" She said quietly, standing with her arms folded.

"Yeah?" He turned at his doorway.

"Did they talk about the transplant while you were out walking around with them?"

"No, not really. Why?"

"I was thinking about what Research 1 said. That maybe Jeff has gone weird because of the shock of waking up and finding out what happened to him. That might throw anybody, don't you think?"

"Sure. What about it?"

"If that's true, then the transplant was actually successful, wouldn't you say? The surgery itself, I mean, and all the adjustments they had to make in the robot body."

"Yeah, I guess so. But they aren't sure that's the case, remember? It's just one possibility." He cocked his head. "Since when did you get interested in all this?"

She shrugged self-consciously. "I was just thinking about it. On account of talking to Jeff. He says it's not too bad."

"Not too bad? Being a robot on the outside and a human on

the inside?" He had started to smirk, teasing her, but then realization crossed his face. "Hey, wait a minute. You don't . . . ?"

"Not for sure." She turned away, embarrassed. "I just want to know more about it, that's all."

"You mean you'd actually consider this? Turning yourself into a robot?"

She nodded her head without turning around.

"And then what—stay here? In this ridiculous place?" His voice was filled with wonder as much as anger.

"It's better than dying!" She whirled on him. "Or being frozen whole and maybe never waking up! What if there isn't any cure, anywhere? Maybe these robots could find one, if I stayed long enough." She felt tears stinging her eyes.

"Well, . . ." He paused uncertainly. "What about the other possibility? Maybe the robots messed up somehow. Maybe that's why Jeff's going crazy. You can't risk that. That would be worse than looking for a cure off the planet somewhere."

"If we get off the planet! Derec, what if we're still stuck here? I won't have anything to lose then, will I?"

"Well, I . . . I don't know. Maybe not."

"And what if Jeff was always a little crazy? Nobody here knows him. Maybe he hasn't been changed at all. What about that?"

He shook his head. "Maybe that's true. You were the one who came up with the theory about his going crazy now. All I know is that if they can't rig up the transplant right, it could kill you faster than your disease."

She looked away from him.

He hesitated, watching her. When she didn't say anything else, he went on into his room.

She walked into her own room and collapsed on her bed to stare at the ceiling. Then she remembered: it would not do her any good. One of the effects of her disease, before causing death, was insanity. Even a transplant like Jeff's would not help her escape her own brain.

CHAPTER 15
THE CIRCLE TIGHTENS

Jeff stood on the stationary shoulder of a slidewalk, at the apex of a high, arching overpass. Robots and vehicles passed on a major boulevard several stories below him. On one corner, five humanoid robots were talking. He had watched three of them approach the other two, and had seen that the pair standing together had blocked their path to engage them in conversation.

He couldn't tell what they were discussing at this distance, but normally robots would communicate privately among themselves through their comlinks. The most likely reason they were using spoken communication was that they were searching for him. His lack of a comlink was one identifying mark he could not disguise.

"You can't go that way, either, Jeffrey," he said into the slight breeze. It would carry his voice the other way, so that even their most sensitive robot hearing would not detect it. "They think they're closing in. Well, maybe they are and maybe they aren't. We'll see."

He stepped onto the slowest lane of the slidewalk and rode it standing still, carefully watching in all directions. With his vision magnified for distances, he was able to spot these little clusters of conversing robots before they noticed him. They were uncharacteristic of normal robot behavior.

As near as he could tell, these clusters were coming toward the center of the city from all directions. They had been slowed down, though, because the population was higher as they approached the heart of the urban area. That might give him time to figure out an escape.

"Time for another reconnoiter, Jeffrey ol' pal. Just keep it casual and don't let anybody sneak up on you. Got it? Of course I've got it, you moron; I'm you." He laughed at his little joke and prepared to change direction at an upcoming junction ramp with another slidewalk.

He knew, by this time, the routes that gave him the most visibility, either with raised sections of slidewalk or open areas that offered a broad vista of the city. The robots involved in the pattern search were direct, and made no attempt to disguise their efforts, so he was able to see how much progress they had made. The circle was surprisingly tight, and still closing in.

"Now it's time to check out their procedure a little more closely. It'll take some care, Jeff. Think you can handle that? Of course I can. Shut up and get to work."

He was hoping to eavesdrop. The difficulty was in listening without attracting the attention of the search team. He continued to ride the slidewalks until he found a cluster of robots speaking below another slidewalk overpass. When he was close enough, he stepped off onto the shoulder again and turned up his aural sensitivity until he could hear them clearly.

"We have contacted all three of you through your comlinks," one robot was saying. "We believe all three of you responded, but we wish to speak aloud with you as well."

"Identify," said another.

"I am Drainage Foreman 31. I am temporarily suspended from my regular duties. At the present time, I am leading this team of three robots in search of a human with the physical body of a robot. This is the purpose of our questions."

An extended moment of silence followed. Jeff understood what was happening. The search team was matching up comlink communication with eye contact and spoken words so that they would have no chance of letting him through by mistake, or by his getting lost in the crowd.

"I am going to repeat my answer to you aloud," Drainage

Foreman 31 said to another robot. "This human had his brain successfully transplanted into the body of a robot. For this reason, he has the strength and appearance of a robot, but the authority of the Laws of Robotics. I am going to ask you a question aloud now. Please respond through your comlink."

Another moment of silence followed, then more talk of a similar kind.

Jeff stepped back onto the slidewalk to ride away. He was convinced that he could not fake having a comlink. That one robot was being very thorough in his testing, and he was backed up by two more robots. Jeff couldn't win a wrestling match with three robots, each with a strength equal to his own.

He was still wary as he approached a tunnel stop. If the robots did not shut down the system entirely, they would at some point stake it out, perhaps with checkpoints down in the tunnels themselves. They could not be careless enough to have forgotten it. However, they might not yet have set up their search there.

"This block is clear so far," he muttered to himself, looking toward a tunnel stop. "And no one's standing at the opening. All right, then. Casually, like before—and watch out for a checkpoint down in the tunnel itself. Right? Of course you're right. So am I. I know you are. Shut up and let's go. Okay, okay. . . ."

He went on muttering to himself, seriously now, as he sauntered toward the stop. Several humanoid robots passed him on the way, as well as the normal crowd of function robots of all sizes and types, but he was not worried about any of them. The search teams had so far all been teams of threes, and they had stopped every humanoid robot they met. They did not just walk around normally, like this.

At the open tunnel stop, he paused to glance around. Everything seemed fine so far. He got on the ramp and rode down into the tunnel. "Maybe your luck will hold, Jeffrey ol' friend. Of course it will; why wouldn't it? Well, just don't get overconfident."

They were after him. He knew they were after him. They had no right to stop him; he hadn't done anything wrong and he hadn't hurt anyone, not even a robot. They were only robots, anyway. They had no reason to be after him.

What if something had gone wrong with them? What if they

didn't have to obey the Laws any more, either? They ran this city by themselves, didn't they? They could change the rules. Surely they manufactured their fellow robots right here. What if they were making positronic brains that didn't obey the Laws? They must be. Otherwise, how could they be chasing him at all? Trying to capture him had to break some Law or other.

That's why they wanted him. He had the same freedom from the Laws, but he wasn't one of them. They had just been pretending to obey the Laws before.

At the base of the ramp, he peered around suspiciously. Nothing appeared out of order around the siding loop. He stepped into one of the booths and punched the keys on the console for his destination.

Nothing happened.

Then a green instruction light appeared, reading, "Temporary adjustment in control system requires use of robotic comlink. Give standard destination code to activate booth."

He sprang out of the booth, then looked around in embarrassment. If a searching robot had seen him fail to activate the booth, he would be identified on the spot. Fortunately, no one had noticed.

So, they had taken his beloved tunnel system away from him. All right. That didn't mean he was finished. After all, they were just robots. He was human— "Right?" He spoke aloud. "Of course you're right. Now shut up before you give yourself away."

He rode up the ramp slowly, glancing in all directions when he reached the surface. "We are still in disguise, still in disguise. Let's approach the enemy's lair and see what we can see. Very good, very good."

Newly resolved to keep quiet for as long as he could remember to do so, he started again for the residence of Derec and Ariel. He knew that they lived near the center of the city, certainly in the central area, and he was guessing that the pattern search was ultimately closing in on that spot. That meant he could escape detection the longest there, and, if he was lucky, he just might overhear something that would let him make a successful getaway.

"Just remember," he said to himself. "Don't let them actually lay eyes on you. They don't seem to tell us robots apart too well, but they just might recognize you, ol' buddy. Right? Right. Shut up; you're talking out loud again."

He recognized the building and the entranceway to their residence easily enough, but he had no plans for what to do next. Since robots did not normally loiter, he could not very well just hang around watching the place.

One of the reasons he had been safe from detection in the tunnel system was that he had been isolated in the booths. Another was that the very act of moving made him appear occupied, like all the legitimate residents of Robot City. He got onto a slidewalk and started walking purposefully, hoping that this would work as an adequate substitute for the time being.

As usual, he set up a route that carried him in an irregular, jagged rotation, now using the human residence as a central reference point. He used the first two circuits to look for search teams, but he didn't see any here. Then he relaxed somewhat and altered his route so that he passed within sight of the human residence more often.

Derec and Ariel did not appear while he was watching. He wondered if he might do better talking to Derec than to Ariel, though she had said she was at least interested in the transplant. She had not been so optimistic about Derec, but maybe she was wrong.

He would not want to talk to Derec yet, since she might be right. If he could talk to her again first, maybe she would have the transplant and understand why it was so desirable. Then they could both convince Derec to join them.

He would just have to wait and watch.

By the time he had lost count of the number of circuits he had made, boredom was setting in. Maybe those two hardly ever came out of their lair. Or maybe they weren't in there at all, but out roaming around the city—looking for him, probably. He laughed—giggling, really—at the idea. If they would just come home, their search would be over.

"No, it wouldn't," he said aloud, sobering suddenly. "I would still have to hide from them. I'd have to be careful, wouldn't I? Of course you would. Now be quiet."

He got off the slidewalk in view of their entranceway, just because he was tired of riding around and around. "A real robot wouldn't get tired of it," he said. "A real robot would just do it over and over until the job was done. But not you. That's why you're still human, isn't it? Huh? Of course it is."

He stood on the shoulder of the slidewalk, wondering what he should do next. "You forgot to tell me to shut up," he added. "All right, shut up. Thank you."

A humanoid robot came riding up on the slidewalk. As he neared Jeff, he stepped off and walked up to him. "Identify," he said. "Use your comlink, please."

"Uh—" Jeff stared at him in shock. This guy was alone, without any search team. Apparently they had altered their policy. Jeff was caught totally off guard. "I, uh—what do you want?"

"I am not receiving you," said the robot. "Please accompany me. I am under instructions to escort all robots without functioning comlinks to a location nearby."

"Do you know why?" Jeff didn't move. He was thinking as fast as he could. If he could stall, he would.

The robot looked at him without speaking. After a moment, Jeff realized the reason.

"Please answer me out loud," said Jeff. "I'm not receiving you, any more than I'm transmitting."

"Yes," said the robot out loud. "I know why."

"Tell me."

"We are searching for Jeff Leong. He is a human brain in a robot body. It possesses no comlink. A secondary benefit may be the identification of robots whose comlinks have malfunctioned without their having noticed, so they can be repaired."

"Identify."

"I am Air Quality Foreman 6."

"Who gave you this instruction?"

"Human Research 1."

"Yeah, I know him. Another robot, in other words."

"Yes. Of course."

"Don't get smart with me, slag heap. Now, then. I know something about robots from when I was on Aurora. If a human gives you an order that contradicts an instruction from a robot, the Second Law makes you obey the human, right?"

"Assuming no other influences pertain, yes."

"Other influences?" Jeff said suspiciously. "Like what? You aren't trying to break the Laws, are you?"

"No, decidedly not. An example of another influence might be prior programming, for instance. Another would be the force of the First Law, which of course takes precedence over the Second and Third. Are you unaware of this? If you are testing me, under what authority are you acting? Identify."

He was trapped, and would have to gamble.

"I'm Jeff Leong, the human-robot you are searching for. Don't contact anyone!" he shouted suddenly. "Did you obey me? I know how fast those positronic brains of yours can work."

"I obeyed you. I started to use my comlink to report locating you, but I aborted it."

"Aha!" Jeff laughed. "So you have to obey me, eh? Well, well."

"Your orders override the instructions I received from Human Research 1, because programming itself was not involved. He gave me a simple instruction. If you issue orders contrary to my programming, I will not obey."

"Hmm. You believed me pretty quick. Are you sure you believe me?" He demanded.

"Yes. I am not capable of lying about this."

"Why do you believe me?"

"If you had a positronic brain, you would not be able to lie to me and say otherwise. Therefore you must be, or possess, the human brain in the robot body."

"Okay, okay, fair enough. Say, why didn't I think of ordering around search robots before? Jeffrey, you're not yourself. That's why." He giggled to himself. "You certainly aren't, are you?"

"Do you have further instructions for me?" asked Air Quality 6, in the same bland voice as before.

"Oh, yeah—you bet. I sure do. The first order is, you don't let on to anyone who I am. Understand? I'm just another robot here in town. Got it?"

"I understand."

"Good. Now we're going to be a team. I'll give you the orders and you'll obey them. Since you have a comlink that works, you're going to help me get away from all these search teams. If you detect the presence of one of those teams, you alert me and help me avoid them. We're going to get out of here. Got it?"

"I understand that we are going somewhere. I do not know what 'here' we are getting out of."

"I'll explain one step at a time," said Jeff, eyeing the robot thoughtfully. "Well, well. I think we're going to get along. You know, taking over this town is going to be easier than I thought. Let's go down to the nearest tunnel stop. You know where it is?"

"Yes. Follow me."

Derec was munching bacon and wiping out the inside of the chemical processor's receptacle when Ariel sat up straight in her chair by the computer console.

"Derec, we've got something. He's been found. Sort of."

"What do you mean, sort of? What is it?" He hurried to her and leaned down to read over her shoulder.

"A partial alert came into the central computer just now. All it says is, 'Jeff Leong located.'"

"That's all? That doesn't sound like an efficient robot message. Move over. I bet the message was aborted somehow—maybe Jeff punched him or something." He leaned in front of her and quickly keyed for the location of the report and read the coordinates. "Hey—that's right outside! Come on!"

He turned and ran out, aware of Ariel following right behind him.

Derec skidded to a stop on the street, looking all around. Various humanoid robots were in sight, but none were doing anything unusual. He had no way of picking out one over another.

"Derec, how about those two?" She pointed at a pair of humanoid robots just going around a corner. "I think that one looks sort of like Jeff, don't you?"

"Could be, I guess. . . . There's a tunnel stop over there. I think I've got it—he's ordered another robot to run the tunnel booths for him. If he does, he can go anywhere. The whole search will be a waste of time. Come on!" He ran back inside and got on the console.

"What are you doing? Shouldn't we try to catch them?"

"We are. Here it is—the destination he's chosen. I see—he's only going a couple of stops from here. He must be pretty sharp. Instead of just heading out as far as he can go, and risking interception, he's going to leave a broken, unpredictable trail. Maybe I can alert some robots in that area, somehow—"

"That's a waste of time!" Ariel shouted. "Look where he's going—it's right next to the Key Center. He still has a distance to go. We can beat him there ourselves!"

"What? How?" Derec turned to look at her, but she was already running out the door. He hesitated, then got up and ran after her.

Jeff and Air Quality 6 had had to squeeze into the same tunnel booth, of course, and it was very crowded. Jeff decided to make this stint a short one, to test Air Quality 6's reliability. He still wondered if some kind of programming might have allowed the robots to act in unusual ways for the sake of trapping him. Air Quality 6 activated the booth, and they took off through the tunnel.

The awkward fit in the booth made the trip seem longer than it was. Finally, they slowed into the siding loop and got out. Jeff led the way up the ramp.

The great bronze dome he had often seen rose up in front of them, gleaming in the sunlight. He didn't know what it was, but it was a visual reference point he had often used. Air Quality 6 had brought him here faithfully, so he supposed he could trust the robot after all.

"Good job, pal," Jeff said to the robot. "Well, I guess we can take a longer trip now, maybe out to the edge of town. You probably know this place better than I do. You got any suggestions?"

"I detect the approach of two humans from one direction and a robot from another."

"What? Where?"

"There." Air Quality 6 pointed to a transparent, horizontal chute lined up with a loading dock not far away. Derec and Ariel were climbing out of the vacuum tube. "And there. The robot is not in sight yet, but is about to come around a corner. He had been using his comlink to contact me."

"You didn't respond, did you?" Jeff growled in a low voice.

"No."

"Good. You freeze—don't speak, move, or communicate in any way till I give you the counter order."

Jeff froze himself into position at the same moment, just as Derec and Ariel came running up.

"Is that you, Jeff?" Ariel asked breathlessly.

Jeff held himself still, and was relieved to see that his last order to Air Quality 6 was being obeyed, as well.

"One of you has a positronic brain," said Derec. "I order that one to answer us. Which one is Jeff?"

Jeff spent a very long moment waiting, but was glad to realize that his order to Air Quality 6 for silence had taken precedence. He might just figure a way out of this problem yet.

"You are Derec and Ariel?" asked another robot, joining them. "I am Assistant Planner 3. I have been participating in the random search for Jeff Leong and received your emergency message from the central computer."

"Thanks for coming," said Derec. "We seem to have a problem here. They aren't responding."

"So I understand. I have been attempting to communicate with them through my comlink ever since I received your message, but I have not had a response, either."

Ariel stood right in front of Jeff and peered into his eyeslit. "I think this one's Jeff. I'm not real good telling these robots apart, but they all have slight differences. This looks like him. You in there, Jeff?"

"All right," said Derec. "This is going to take some effort. We'll have to get them together with the other robots whose comlinks don't work; I understand that two or three more have been found. Assistant Planner 3, please arrange for this. Make sure the medical team joins us."

CHAPTER 16
SIMON SAYS

Five suspect robots were taken to the Human Experimental Facility. Two were frozen into position and completely uncommunicative. The other three were mobile, apparently cooperative, and could speak aloud.

As Derec and Ariel entered the building, she shook her head and said, "I'm sure that one is Jeff. We really don't have to waste time on the others."

"I'm not doubting you," said Derec. "I'm certain that one of those two is Jeff. The problem is that their bodies are the same model, so the medical team can't tell them apart, and I'm not sure you can, either. In any case, it appears that we'll have to smoke him out to make him admit which one he is."

"Welcome to our facility," said Research 1. "Please follow me down the hall. We have the suspect robots here waiting for you. It is large enough to accommodate everyone."

He led them into a room from which all furniture and equipment had been removed. From the marks on the floor, Derec saw that it had been cleared for this project. The five suspects were standing in a line against one wall.

"Derec," said one of them.

He looked up in surprise. "Alpha? Alpha, is that you?" He laughed and walked over to the one robot whose physical details were unique, suppressing an impulse to embrace him. "*Hi*. How did you get here?"

"Hi," said Alpha. "I was able to obtain a very small spacecraft and trace the source of the asteroid-disassembling operation to this planet. Wolruf accompanied me. More recently, I was detained by a robot search team and brought here."

"Spacecraft?" Derec suppressed a giggle of delight and caught Ariel's eye. "And Wolruf, too. How is she?"

"She is recovering from a difficult trip."

"Recovering?" Ariel said. "But she'll be all right?"

"Yes."

"I'm glad," said Derec. "We've worried about her. We'll want to see her when we can. What about the spacecraft? Does it still work? And is it here and available and all that?"

"Yes."

"Step out of line, Alpha." Derec turned, grinning to the medical team. "This is not Jeff. I put Alpha together myself."

"Hi, Alpha," said Ariel, bouncing on the balls of her feet in excitement. "I'm real glad to see you. But why did they stop you? You have a comlink, don't you."

"Greetings, Katherine. My comlink was originally set at a slightly different frequency. I altered it but was detained anyway, I believe for having an anomalous comlink."

"I'm Ariel Welsh now."

"I do not understand," said Alpha.

"Not now, not now. We'll catch up with each other later," said Derec. "For the business at hand, we're down to four," said Derec, looking over the others. "Research 1, were you able to begin testing, like you said?"

"Yes. According to our standard maintenance scanning procedure on their bodies, all four are in good condition, other than their common lack of functioning comlinks. Their heads have not been scanned. The two speaking robots have given identification that has been verified by the central computer. Their comlinks simply malfunctioned."

"Dismiss them," said Derec. "Alpha, you stay right here until further notice."

"Report to the nearest repair facility," said Research 1.

The other two robots left.

"So." Derec stood in front of the two remaining robots, looking back and forth between them. "One of you is almost certainly Jeff. Unless you've fallen asleep, which I really doubt under the circumstances, you can hear me and you just aren't letting on. Well, we'll be right back." He turned away, then paused to grin over his shoulder. "Don't go anywhere, now. You'll give yourself away."

"Surgeon 1, you stay and watch them. Research, you and Ariel step outside with me for a minute."

Derec paused in the hall, but Research 1 shook his head. "This is not sufficient for privacy. If you want to talk privately, we must go into another room and I will create sonic camouflage. Do not forget that Jeff has robotic hearing."

"Lead the way." Derec could hardly keep from dancing around with joy. Alpha had a working spacecraft somewhere here—once he and Ariel had smoked out Jeff, they could turn him over to the robots and take off. As they followed Research 1 into another room, he saw the smile on Ariel's face and nudged her playfully with his elbow. She elbowed him back, a lot harder, but still grinning.

They entered what was obviously the facility's operating room. Research 1 flipped a switch on some sort of scanning apparatus and a faint hum came on.

"They will not hear us. What do you wish to discuss?" Research 1 asked.

"They?" Ariel asked. "I don't get it. One of them is an inoperative robot, isn't he?"

"Immobile is not necessarily inoperative," said Research 1. "We must be cautious."

"Exactly," said Derec. "Here's how I figure it so far—correct me if I'm off. Jeff saw us coming in time to order another robot to freeze, and probably to follow only his instructions to activate again. I did basically the same thing with Alpha once. However, in order to hear Jeff's instruction to reactivate, the other robot has to maintain hearing sensitivity and at least some mental activity. Right?"

"Correct," said Research 1.

"What about a shortcut?" Derec asked. "Can't you just scan their heads and find out which has the biological brain in it?"

"No," said Research 1. "In constructing his special cranium, we used materials that would be extremely resistant to the entrance of any forms of energy, as well as to physical impact. Turning up our scanning beams to a strength that would penetrate his cranium would endanger the brain inside."

"Hold it," said Ariel. "You could use your normal scanning beam, and when you get a reading for one positronic brain and one null reading, we'd know by elimination."

"We dare not," said Research 1. "The cranium was tested before use, but not with the human brain inside. Even the normal scanning beam could be dangerous. The First Law does not allow us to take a risk of this magnitude."

"All right. Somehow, I'm not surprised." Derec sighed.

"The Laws of Robotics still hold precedence on them, too, though," said Ariel. "I assume our tests will still work—won't they?"

"Yes. They are based on the following," said Research 1. "If Jeff had a positronic brain, he would have to obey the Laws—for instance, if one of you were in danger, he would have to save you. However, as a human, he could allow you to come to harm if he wished."

"The problem," said Derec, "is that Jeff knows the Laws and can masquerade as a robot."

"We also don't know what he told the other robot," said Ariel. "If the other robot knows that we are setting up tests, then he won't believe we're really in danger and he won't have to obey the Laws, either. They'll still behave the same way."

"Let's get started and see what happens," said Derec. "We'll go in order, with tests one, two, and three."

Derec and Ariel went back into the room with the suspect robots. The medical team had to leave, accompanied by Alpha, in order to avoid confusion. If they did not respond according to the Laws, the real robot would see it was a test; if they did respond, they would get in the way.

"I've had it with you," Derec was yelling at Ariel. "You're crazy." He turned toward her in front of both robots.

"Oh, yeah?" She demanded. Then, according to their agreement, she swung back her fist and punched him in the stomach.

Even though he had been expecting the blow, Derec doubled over from the impact—partly from her very solid punch and partly as an act. Both robots jumped forward, no longer frozen in place, and pulled them apart. If one had been a shade faster, he couldn't tell.

"Let go of me! Him, too!" Ariel shouted, as they had prearranged. Both robots obeyed, but remained between them, close enough to prevent more violence.

Derec, gasping for breath, looked up and found that they had both apparently deactivated again. It was time for the second test. He caught Ariel's eye, saw that she was ready for him, and leaped at her throat as if to strangle her.

Instantly, both robots grabbed him in their powerful arms and held him fixed and helpless.

"Let go of me," he ordered.

Neither one let him go. Now that the violence had been repeated, the First Law was going to remain in force over the Second, until they judged that the threat was over.

"You," Ariel ordered, tapping one on the arm. "You go stand in the hall. The other one will keep me safe here. And you—Derec won't hurt me right now. I know that. You can stand close if it makes you feel better, to stop us again if necessary."

When both robots had complied, Derec and Ariel spoke amiably to demonstrate that the immediate threat of violence was over. Then the robots allowed them to retreat to the O.R. once again to consult with each other.

"Jeff's pretty good," said Derec. "He was right with the real robot every second—whichever one it was." He grinned. "You've got a pretty good punch."

Ariel shrugged. "Well, you said it should be the real thing. But now we know a little more. Direct application of the Laws activates the real robot, but only as long as the Laws apply. Then he freezes again, like Jeff ordered him."

"We'd better keep them separate. If Jeff is picking up his cue by watching the other robot, he'll never mess up."

"Good idea. Ready for test three?"

"Let's go," he said.

In the hallway, Surgeon 1 handed him a small gray cylinder that fit conveniently into his hand. It was an intermediate laser scalpel, used for certain types of repair on robot bodies, capable of cutting through any portion of a robot body. Derec hefted it, shifted it comfortably, and held it up as he entered the testing room.

"I'm going to cut your leg off with this," he said to the

suspect robot. "In return for your interfering with me." He turned it up to full power, stood where he was, and aimed the beam at the robot's knee joint. "The Third Law says you can't allow this to happen. Right?"

The robot slid to one side, avoiding the beam. Derec followed him with it, and the robot moved away again. When Derec started shooting at his legs in spurts, like it was a gun, the robot danced around, backing up, dodging, watching the beam intently.

"I'll get you," Derec growled. "Ha! Close. Ha! Again. Almost. Ha! Hold still! I'll take your leg off—"

The robot continued to shuffle away from the beam with its quick and reliable robot reflexes.

Derec laughed triumphantly and shut off the laser. "Got you, Jeff. An old Simon Says trick—remember that game? I ordered you to hold still, and in the heat of the moment, you forgot that the Second Law takes precedence over the Third. You didn't hold still!"

The robot in front of him had frozen again, but now Derec was certain.

"You can't fool me now; it's too late. A positronic brain wouldn't forget the order of the Laws for even a second, under any circumstances." Derec called in everyone else and explained the situation.

"This is convincing to me," said Research 1. "Since the other suspect is by elimination almost certain to be a true robot, we can verify beyond any doubt by sending him to a repair facility."

"Research 1," Surgeon 1 said warningly.

"I will escort him," said Research 1. "The repair crews must be very cautious, in the event that we are mistaken. They must understand the situation, so that no Laws will be violated."

Derec jerked his thumb at Jeff. "We know who he is, but until he quits play-acting, we can't have much of a dialogue."

Ariel caught his eye and inclined her head toward the door. Derec followed her out and they returned to the O.R. to talk. Surgeon 1 remained with Jeff.

"Maybe we can sucker him," said Ariel.

"All right. How?"

"Loosen the watch on him. He's still trying to play-act being a robot because there's a microscopic chance that a positronic brain could have malfunctioned this way. But if he tries to escape, he'll have to admit we know."

A few minutes later, everyone gathered in the testing room again in front of Jeff, except for the robot still motionless in the hall.

"We've decided to move on to the next phase," said Derec. "Research 1, please escort the other robot to be repaired."

Research 1 left the room.

"Now," said Derec. "Alpha, please leave the room but remain out in the hall—at the end of the hall, out of the way. We definitely have to talk to you."

"Yes, Derec." Alpha left.

"Surgeon 1," said Ariel. "We are no longer completely sure that this robot is really Jeff. Return to your regular duties in the facility. Derec and I are going to have to figure out what to do next."

"Very well." Surgeon 1 left the room.

Derec casually put his arm around Ariel and walked her toward the door. "Maybe we should get something to eat and relax a little. Then we can work out our next move."

Ariel closed the door behind them. Alpha was waiting motionless at the far end of the hall; they went out the front door, in the opposite direction. Without speaking, since they didn't know how well Jeff could hear, they walked outside and looked around.

The Human Experimental Facility was a simple rectangular block. It had none of the striking geometric design of most of Robot City; with their usual efficiency, the robots had built it without frills. Derec saw nowhere to hide except around the corner.

They sat down on the pavement just around one corner, still silent, by prior arrangement. Jeff was likely to be cautious, so they knew they could have a long wait. Surgeon 1, also by agreement, had taken up his "regular duties" in a room across from the testing room. With his own robotic hearing, he also was waiting for Jeff to make his escape.

Derec found himself grinning in anticipation of using Alpha's spacecraft. They could help the robots take care of Jeff, of course, but now that they could look forward to leaving when the job was done, waiting didn't seem so bad. He looked at Ariel, who was also smiling when she turned to him. With suppressed laughter, they didn't have to talk to feel close.

The day wore on, and Jeff's patience was at least as good as theirs. Derec did notice that Ariel seemed as content as he was to keep waiting. He kept thinking that he would soon go somewhere and find out who he was, or even find a cure for his amnesia. Maybe she was dreaming of finding her own cure off the planet.

Finally, a single, moderately loud robotic shout went up inside the facility: "Derec!"

He recognized Surgeon 1's voice, and jumped up with Ariel. Around the corner, Jeff was just now walking out the front door with controlled, casual steps.

"Got you!" yelled Derec, pointing at him. "Give it up." He and Ariel ran up to block Jeff's way.

Jeff reached for them both with his powerful robot arms. He was free of the First Law, but Surgeon 1 wasn't, and he leaped on Jeff from behind, pinning his arms back.

"Alpha!" Derec called. "Come out here!"

"Release me," Jeff yelled at Surgeon 1, pulling and jerking to no effect.

"You may not harm them or yourself," Surgeon 1 answered.

"I have no intention of harming anyone," Jeff shouted angrily. "I order you to release me."

"Hold him, Doc," said Ariel, keeping her distance.

Derec saw that Surgeon 1 was hesitating, probably experiencing a positronic conflict from the fact that Jeff had never really shown a desire to harm anyone. The weight of conflicting human orders was otherwise near neutral. Before, and now, he had only pushed them so that he could get away.

"Release me and freeze," ordered Jeff. He wrenched himself free and started to run.

Surgeon 1 had not frozen, but he was moving slowly, uncertainly, as he worked through the conflicting human orders.

"Alpha!" Derec shouted, seeing him emerge from the building. "That's Jeff. He needs medical care and doesn't know it. First Law applies—stop him!"

In surprise, Jeff paused to look back. Surgeon 1 was again galvanized to action by the First Law application, since it overrode the problems of the Second Law. He tackled Jeff around the knees as Alpha ran up to pinion his arms.

Jeff's robot fist swung low and jerked back Surgeon 1's head. He also raised a knee and then kicked upward, throwing Alpha back. Surgeon 1 held on, though, preventing him from getting away.

As the three robot bodies wrestled and thrashed together, Derec saw the difficulty: Alpha and Surgeon 1 could only subdue Jeff without risking any damage to him, and in the confusion of combat, they were being particularly careful, since no one had ever really tested the cranial protection around Jeff's brain. On the other hand, Jeff was free to smash, twist, and rip at their bodies in any way he thought would get him free.

Derec skipped helplessly around the three tussling bodies. With two opponents, Jeff could not get free, but with the unequal restrictions placed on them, the other two could not pin him down, either. Ariel looked from them to Derec questioningly—then turned and ran, looking for more help.

Now Alpha was lying flat on his back, with Jeff trying to get up off him while Surgeon 1 again had his arms pinned behind him. Jeff managed to get one of his legs under him, and struggled to stand. Alpha's standard arm was caught beneath his body, and Jeff was still gripping his other one above the elbow.

His other one.

"Alpha," shouted Derec. "Make your arm flexible—loosen it up. Use it however you need to in order to stop him!"

Instantly, Alpha's arm lost its elbow entirely and became a fully flexible coil. The hand curved back and tightened on Jeff's wrist to pull it free. Then the arm curved around, locking the joints on Jeff's arm to make it immobile.

Surgeon 1 released Jeff's arms and encircled his knees. Alpha and Surgeon 1 stood up and finally held Jeff immobile, off the ground, as Ariel ran up with a couple of other robots she had commandeered with an emergency First Law appeal.

Jeff was still thrashing about in his captors' arms. "You slag heaps! You traitorous can heads! You can't hold me! I'm human, you understand? Let go of me! Now! I order you to put me down!"

"Can you sedate him?" Derec asked. "You can't just hang onto him this way while we figure out what to do next. Making him sleep wouldn't be harming him."

"I will sedate him," said Surgeon 1, still holding Jeff's legs with effort. "We are making progress, I believe. When Research 1 returns, we must consult on the matter of treatment. I experienced a moment of hesitation while in physical conflict just now over a First Law question that must be addressed." He took a step backward, reacting to a convulsive kick by Jeff. The other robots took hold as well, assuring that the cyborg could not escape.

"I'll kill you! I'll melt you all down!" Jeff screamed. "Just wait till I'm in charge!" He thrashed and kicked again.

"Go ahead and do what you need to," said Derec. "We'll hang around; don't worry about that."

"Into the O.R.," said Surgeon 1. He and the others trooped inside the building, carrying their screaming cargo.

Derec let out a sigh of relief and turned to Ariel, ready to make some kind of joke. He stopped when he saw the look of disappointment on her face.

Jeff woke up in dim light again, but this time he recognized the room. He was not connected to any monitors now, though. His eyes adjusted quickly; he was used to that now, too, and didn't really notice it. He felt firm restraints of some sort holding him in place.

So they had him again. His memory was clear enough—with the bunch of robots forcing him down, Surgeon 1 had somehow introduced a substance into his neck. Jeff supposed it had gone into one of the nutrient avenues to his brain. In any case, he had been sleeping, and still felt drowsy and languid.

He was alone in the room, which was silent, but he could hear faint noises beyond the walls. His enemies were probably holding a meeting of some sort. By concentrating, he was able to turn up his aural acuity, and just make out some familiar voices.

"The First Law problem I experienced was this," said Surgeon 1. "We have reason to believe that the transplantation of Jeff's brain into a robot body has adversely affected him. If so, then the First Law requires that we undo the transplant, once we have scanned Derec for the knowledge we need to repair Jeff's body."

"So what's the problem?" Ariel asked.

"The problem is Jeff's resistance," said Surgeon 1. "We are not certain that the transplant has adversely affected him. Without the imperative of the First Law, we cannot transplant his brain—or even test him—without his permission."

"And he certainly doesn't seem inclined to give it," Derec observed. "There's not much doubt about that."

Jeff muttered to himself, "You're right about that, frost head. You're absolutely right about that. You want to take my body away from me again? You want to make me into a weakling again, like you? Stop me from taking over this planet? Ha."

"When is he due to wake up?" asked Research 1.

"Any time now," said Surgeon 1.

"Then I suggest, first, that we be more cautious in discussing him, since he may hear us," said Research 1, "and, second, that we consult with him and make certain that he understands our position."

"Good idea," said Derec. "Alpha, you and Wolruf stay here. That room won't hold all of us comfortably."

The moment the door opened, letting in a shaft of bright white light, Jeff shouted, "Let me out of here! You have no right to hold me prisoner—none of you do! Now let me up!"

They lined up at the foot of his bed, shoulder to shoulder, watching him in silence: Research 1 and Surgeon 1 on the left, and Derec and Ariel on the right.

"Frost! Don't you understand your own Laws?" Jeff demanded of the robots.

"Yes," said both robots in unison. They looked anxiously at Derec and Ariel.

"It's not that simple, Jeff," said Derec. "Look, there's a possibility that a medical problem—"

"Sure it is," Jeff growled. "I want to get up and out. That's very simple. So, let me up and out. What are you after me for, anyway? I didn't do anything."

"You're not yourself, Jeff," said Ariel sympathetically. "A little while ago, you were shouting about taking over. You remember talking to me through some sort of broadcasting link? You told me we could be very powerful here. But I don't think that's really you."

"It is now," Jeff said haughtily. "They created the new me,

and now this *is* me. And you have no right to make me over again."

"All they really need at this stage," said Derec, "is to run some tests on you. They want to find out if there's a chemical imbalance in your brain that they caused—"

"Making me crazy? Is that it? You telling me I've gone crazy? I'm not stupid; I'll tell you that much. I know you want to get rid of me. You don't like having someone as powerful as I am around, do you? Huh?" Jeff laughed triumphantly, and loudly.

"Jeff," said Ariel. "They have to act according to the Laws, and they can't do that fully unless they run their tests. That way, they'll know exactly where you stand."

"Frost!" Jeff yelled angrily. "If they have to obey the Laws, then why don't they let me go when I tell them to? Huh?"

"Their responsibility is larger than that," said Derec. "Since they put you in this condition, the Laws demand that they make sure you're really okay. The tests alone won't hurt you any, or change you."

"Oh, yeah? How do I know that? Huh?" Jeff looked around at them all. "Supposedly this transplant couldn't hurt me, either, only now you're all saying they might have made a mistake. Well, what if they make another one? What about that?"

Derec glanced at the robots, who said nothing.

"Let's leave him alone for a while," said Derec. "Come on."

Before they left, Research 1 turned on one of the machines in the room. Jeff understood its purpose. The white noise would drown out his ability to eavesdrop any more.

When Jeff was alone again, with the door closed, he tested his restraints. He couldn't see what they were, since he was flat on his back, but they were stronger than he was. If he was going to get out of this untouched by the robots, he would have to argue his way out.

Somehow.

Back in the testing room, Derec turned to his companions with an exaggerated shrug. "Well? Now what?"

"I regret to interrupt," said Alpha, "but I must inform you of a fundamental change in my identity."

"What?" Derec turned to him. "What are you talking about?"

"At the time you instructed me to use my cellular arm, I experienced a signal from it changing my designation from Alpha to Mandelbrot."

"Mandelbrot?" Ariel said. "Why?"

"I do not know."

"What does it mean?" Derec asked. He was annoyed at the interruption in his train of thought about Jeff, but he could not ignore the mystery.

"It means nothing other than a name change to me," said Mandelbrot.

"And it came from your cellular arm at the time I gave you the order to use it." Derec thought a moment. "It was encoded in your arm when I found the part, then. Using your flexibility triggered the signal. . . ."

"Could it be a safety measure of some kind?" Ariel asked. "Maybe a warning. This whole planet seems to be programmed with fear and security in mind. His arm came from an Avery robot on that asteroid, didn't it?"

"That's right," said Derec. "I don't know exactly what the signal means. Perhaps it was triggered by the combined use of some Avery parts and some standard robot parts together." He looked at Ariel. "Maybe it means another signal has been sent out to call Avery back."

"If he's alive."

"Yeah." Derec shook his head. "First things first. Let's get back to Jeff."

"That theory is consistent with another important change in me," said Mandelbrot.

"What is it?" Derec asked impatiently.

"My store of data pertinent to the location of this planet was erased at the time of the name change."

Derec and Ariel both turned to him.

"How important is that?" Derec demanded. "You can still program a ship away from here to a major spacelane, can't you?"

"Given the considerable length of spacelanes, I believe so. However, this memory erasure suggests that the signal from my arm was definitely related to the security and isolation of this planet."

"Good point," said Derec, "but once we leave this place, I'm not going to care. Let's get back to Jeff."

• • •

"I surmise that your visit was not productive," said Mandel-brot. "May I assist you in any way?"

"I haven't thought of how yet," said Derec. "The trouble so far is that the robots can't treat him without permission, and Ariel and I, who don't need permission, don't have the skill to treat him. Anybody have any suggestions?" He looked around at all of them.

"Is there anything we can do to prove that Jeff is out of his head?" Ariel asked. Then she covered her mouth in embarrass-ment. "Sorry. Didn't mean to phrase it that way."

Derec smiled wryly. "We're all under a strain."

"I cannot think of anything," said Research 1. "The kind of unmistakable scientific evidence we require to reach a conclu-sion is only available through a direct analysis of his physical condition."

"Frost, Derec!" Ariel turned to Research 1. "How about us? Can you teach us to help just a little? If we extracted samples of fluid for you, and you analyzed them afterward—would that be acceptable?"

Research 1 hesitated just long enough to reveal some doubt behind his answer. "The acceptability of that arrangement would ultimately rest on how skillful you became. Drawing a sample of synthetic blood would not be difficult, I believe. However, he does not have much margin for error. Unlike natu-rally evolved biological bodies, Jeff's robot body has almost exactly the amount of fluid he requires. Taking too much could be fatal."

"You could make extra," said Derec. "Give him a transfusion while the procedure is going on."

"You would have to administer the transfusion, as well," said Surgeon 2. "And you would have to avoid flooding his system as well as starving it. Nor could you risk mixing the new fluid with the old, or the analysis would be worthless. At this point, we have confronted more complex procedures, including con-stant study and understanding of the monitors. We would be in violation of the First Law if we allowed Jeff to take significant risks in this manner."

Derec nodded, though he was disappointed. "I can't argue with that. The truth is, I'm not sure I'm ready for responsibility over his life that way, myself."

Ariel sighed. "Then we need the permission of a crazy guy. Any idea how to get it?"

Jeff wasn't tired, really, but he had closed his eyes and rested for lack of anything else he could do. He was imprisoned by enemies who were afraid of his power, but he had not given up hope. He could afford to be charitable, once he had taken over.

He opened his eyes at the sound of the door opening, but when he looked, he couldn't see anyone. Then the door closed again. He stiffened at a faint padding sound on the floor.

"Who's there?" He demanded suspiciously.

"Iss Wolruf," said an odd voice.

"What?"

The caninoid alien climbed gently onto the foot of the bed. She had been near death by starvation the only other time he had seen her. Now her mottled brown and gold fur was full and glossy, and her eyes alert and bright. She was perhaps the size of a large dog, such as a small St. Bernard, but her face was flat, without an extended snout, and her ears stood high and pointed. Instead of paws, she had clumsy looking gray-skinned fingers on what he supposed were hands.

"My name iss Wolruf to 'umans. Iss really—" She made an unpronounceable noise and bared her teeth in what might have been a playful smile.

"Wolruf?"

"I came to thank 'u for 'aving me fed," said Wolruf. "Alpha told me 'u saved my life."

"Yeah? Now what do you want?"

"Want nothing," said Wolruf. "Thank 'u."

Jeff watched her for a moment. "You okay now? Is that— Alpha?—taking care of you properly?"

"Everything iss fine."

"He just didn't know how to handle this town, did he?"

"No. Iss strangrr even herr in city of robots."

"Wait a minute. I remember now. I get it. These other robots didn't have to help because you aren't human."

"Iss true."

Jeff laughed in his still-unfamiliar robot voice. "Yes, yes, Jeffrey. This city belongs to you. Only you can see the needs of people here. You can do what no one else here can." He caught Wolruf's eye. "Right? Huh? You should know."

She blinked mildly at him.

"Huh? Right?" He insisted.

"Rright," she said. "But I'm worried."

"Oh?" Jeff said airily. "Anything else I can help with?"

"Worried about my friend."

Jeff hesitated. "Yeah? Who?"

"'U," said Wolruf, nodding at him.

He started to retort, but Wolruf's quiet sincerity stopped him.

"'Urr my first new friend herr," said Wolruf. "Saved my life. Don't want 'u 'urt."

"Everybody says that," said Jeff, but he seemed to lack the same angry suspicion that he had felt before.

"'U saved my life," Wolruf repeated.

"I guess I did. Are you saying you want to repay me?"

Her caninoid shoulders twitched in a sort of furry shrug. "Won't force 'u."

"You may be the first follower I have," Jeff said wonderingly. "Robots have to obey me. Derec and Ariel haven't really . . . come around yet, you might say. What are you worried about, anyhow?"

"'U could be sick."

Jeff stiffened. "Sick? How can I be sick, when I haven't got a normal body?"

"'Urr brain could be sick." She nodded. "Could be. Could be fine."

"They sent you in here, didn't they? To change my mind."

"No. They'rr too busy to remembrr Wolruf. Forgot about me. I just walked away while they werr talking. Came to see 'u."

"Really?" Jeff was surprised. "Just to see me?"

"'U've been alone on Robot City. Only one of 'urr kind. I know about that. 'U could be sick and can't tell. Could find out."

Jeff looked up at the ceiling. He had been feeling lonely, now that she mentioned it. Maybe he was sick.

"I don't trust them," he said to Wolruf. "I can take over this city—this whole planet. They want to stop me." The fire was gone, though; he felt it himself. He was tired, emotionally tired.

"Robots can't 'urt 'u on purpose," she reminded him. "Make rare mistakes, but can't 'urt 'uman on purpose."

"Dcrcc and Ariel—"

"Robots can't allow them to 'urt 'u, either. Test can tell 'u if 'urr sick or not."

Jeff closed his eyes and sighed.

Derec hadn't seen Wolruf leave the group in the testing room, but he noticed her come back in. The little alien bore her distinctive teeth-baring grin when she looked up at him.

"What is it, Wolruf?" He asked.

"Jeff changed 'is mind. Will take test now."

Everyone turned to look at her.

"Are you certain?" asked Research 1.

"I've underestimated you before," said Derec. "Remind me not to do it again."

"Wolruf? How did you manage that?" Ariel asked in astonishment.

"Just talked to 'im," said Wolruf. "Suggest 'u don't talk to 'im, or 'e'll change 'is mind."

"We'll take your word for it," said Derec. "Research 1, you and Surgeon 1 go ahead and run your tests. I suggest that you also conduct a minimum of conversation with him. I guess he's still pretty unpredictable."

"I will begin the procedures with Jeff," said Research 1. "May I request that you allow Surgeon 1 to conduct the scans of your body that we have already discussed? The equipment is prepared, and the central computer will benefit from the information regardless of Jeff's condition and wishes."

"Sure." Derec turned to Ariel and Mandelbrot. "As soon as I'm finished—"

"Right. We'll be here," she said with a grin. "Wolruf, too."

Derec followed Surgeon 1 into a cramped room and stretched out, undressed, on a cold platform at the robot's bidding. The robot attached a variety of sensors to him, all connected to some of the worst looking jury-rigged equipment Derec had seen on this planet. For once, the necessity for speed had overcome the values of minimalist engineering; the robots had put together something that would work, ignoring convenience and appearance.

As Surgeon 1 ran various vibrations through parts of his body and shot him with invisible rays, Derec assured himself that once the emergency with Jeff was past, they would either improve the engineering of this equipment or discard it altogether. They weren't likely to allow an anomaly like this to remain as it was. Still, he felt a sense of petty satisfaction in seeing that they weren't always perfect.

When the scans were finished, Derec got dressed as Surgeon 1 glanced over the monitors.

"This is sufficient," said Surgeon 1. "We are capable of restoring Jeff's body to a state of health, granted his normal recuperative powers after surgery. Research 1 has contacted me through his comlink, and requests our presence back in the testing room."

Research 1 was waiting when they got there.

"Well?" Derec said. "How is he?"

"Ariel's theory appears to be correct. The level of several hormones that can affect mood and behavior in humans were higher than we had intended. Given the limited blood supply, very small amounts skew the percentages."

"I was sure he wasn't that bad a guy," said Ariel.

"Me, too," said Wolruf.

"What are you going to do, though?" Derec asked. "Have you discussed this with him yet?"

"No. Surgeon 1 and I must confer over the details. If Surgeon 1 agrees with me, then Jeff Leong is not responsible for his behavior. In that event, we would take the position that our judgment of his condition under the First Law would override all his orders to us under the Second Law."

"Whew," said Ariel. "That's a very big step."

"I think," said Derec, "that it's time for us to take care of some personal business. Research 1, do you need further human assistance at the moment? If not, we have an important errand to run."

"We do not require your assistance at this time," said Research 1. "I request your return later in the day."

"No problem." Derec turned to Mandelbrot with a big grin. "Okay, friend. Show us this spacecraft you have waiting. I'll have to check its condition and facilities and all. Where is it?"

"It is in a rural area just outside the urban perimeter. One of the tunnels will take us close to the spot."

"Let's go—you, Wolruf, Ariel and me."

The trip out to the perimeter was uneventful, except for the glow of excitement that Derec and Ariel shared. Once they reached the construction perimeter, they had to start hiking. Fortunately, Mandelbrot had chosen a broad, open field for his landing, with only a short cushion of broad-bladed, blue ground cover.

"I see it!" Ariel shouted, pointing to a sliver of blue-silver glinting in the sunlight. It was just beyond a gentle rise in the terrain.

Derec looked up eagerly, then felt a sudden weight of disappointment, even though it was still mostly out of sight. He didn't say anything, though, until they had topped the rise and were looking down on the sleek, undamaged craft. Ariel, too, stopped in surprise.

"It's a lifepod," Derec said dully. It was so small that even the gently rolling ground had hidden it almost completely.

"Correct," said Mandelbrot. "A somewhat converted lifepod. I modified it."

"Alpha," said Derec, shaking his head. "Mandelbrot, I mean."

"I detect distress," said Mandelbrot. "What is its cause?"

"Whatever your name is," Ariel wailed, "we wanted to get out of here. But this little ship only has room for one."

"I traveled with 'im," said Wolruf.

"Mandelbrot, why didn't you tell us it could only carry one full-sized humanoid?" Derec asked. "I asked you where it was, what condition it was in, and so on."

"The only subject of discussion at that time was the welfare of Jeff Leong. I surmised that you wanted it for his use. It is adequate for that purpose."

"Yeah." Derec sighed. "So it is." He slipped an arm casually around Ariel's shoulders. "I think it's more important to get Ariel off the planet, though. She has—something to take care of."

She took his hand and squeezed it, probably for not mentioning her disease in particular.

"How did you modify it?" Derec asked.

"I was able to give it a significant drive ability. Also, I was able to create space for Wolruf. I myself used the space principally intended for human use, but of course I do not have the supply requirements. The supply space was available for her provisions."

Derec nodded, staring silently at the little ship.

No one else spoke. They all seemed to understand the realization, and what it meant to him. Finally, when he turned away, they followed him back to the tunnel stop without a word.

By the time they returned to the facility, Research 1 and Surgeon 1 were just leaving the O.R.

"Are you finished already?" Ariel asked in surprise. "How is he?"

"The procedures have apparently been successful so far," said Surgeon 1. "Unlike the transplantation into his robot body, which required no recovery period, his human body will require an extended recuperative phase with close attention from us."

"The most important unknown factor now is his biological recuperative power, with which we have little experience," said Research 1. "However, we—"

"You think he'll be okay," Derec interpreted. "Right?"

"Correct," said Research 1.

"What about his, well, his attitude?" Ariel asked. "Will his emotional state be normal again?"

"We will have to wait for data about that question. He will sleep for many hours, yet," said Surgeon 1. "We will also have him mildly tranquilized when he first awakens. to guard against further shock when he finds himself fully human again."

"If his body is truly recovering," said Research 1, "his serum levels in all cases should gradually return to normal. I surmise that the effect will not be immediate, but our information is poor on this subject."

Ariel nodded.

"We'll be moving along," said Derec. "I'm going to get on the central computer and see about refurbishing a certain little spacecraft. Also, how many further modifications it might take. Keep us up to date on Jeff through my console, all right?"

CHAPTER 18
LIFT-OFF

Derec was able to assemble a work crew of function robots to take care of the spacecraft under Mandelbrot's direction. The computer released them from normal duty with the understanding that Ariel's welfare would be aided by her leaving the planet. It was not exactly a clear First Law requirement, but in the absence of significant objections, it was sufficient.

Derec was disappointed to learn that the ship would not support the modifications required to support a second human passenger, but he was not surprised. The entire craft was just too small. He and Ariel had watched the robots construct a hangar near where Mandelbrot had landed it, in which minor repairs could be made. He followed the robots' progress with a certain intellectual interest.

Ariel did not seem to like talking about the ship, or where she would go in it. He understood that Aurora was off-limits, and neither of them really knew where she might reasonably look for a cure. Anyway, she wouldn't discuss it.

She brightened for the first time when Research 1 called through the computer console. He told Derec that Jeff was alert, talking, and no longer drugged, for the first time since his body had been restored. She insisted that she and Derec visit him right away.

They found Jeff lying on an air cushion, wearing a soft, loose gown that billowed gently around him. Research 1 had told them that Jeff was self-conscious about the numerous scars he now bore, though they could be largely eliminated by further procedures later on. Derec looked at Jeff's slender body and Asian face and thought he looked more as though he was Derec's age than eighteen.

Jeff's dark eyes darted back and forth suspiciously between them. He said nothing.

"How are you?" Ariel asked.

Jeff looked at her without speaking for a long moment. "Human," he said quietly. "I guess."

"Feeling better?" Derec asked.

Jeff shrugged shyly.

"Are you angry?" Ariel asked.

"About what?" Jeff said cautiously.

Derec looked uncomfortably at Ariel. He hadn't spoken to Jeff as often as she had, and didn't know how to approach him.

"You're not a robot any more," she said.

Jeff shook his head almost imperceptibly. "I, uh . . . feel like I've been in a fog, or something. Like I've been dreaming. Almost like it wasn't real. I remember it, I guess. . . ." He looked up at them both sharply, watching for their reactions.

Derec looked at Ariel again.

"You think I'm lying?" Jeff's voice had a hint of familiar belligerence. "You think I'm just trying to duck responsibility, I suppose. Why don't you get out of here?"

"Come on," Ariel said quietly, tugging at Derec's sleeve. "Let's leave him alone."

Ariel led Derec into what had been the testing room. The original equipment had been put back into it, but it was still an adequate place to talk, especially since Jeff no longer had robotic hearing.

"We have to send him, not me," Ariel said bluntly.

"What?" Derec straightened in surprise.

"He's got to be the one to go."

"He can wait, just like I'll have to. Ariel, you're the one who needs a cure. If Jeff knew that, he might not object, either."

"Derec, did you see how he looked at us? He's not over his—ordeal. He still thinks we're out to get him in some way."

"If you go, then he and I will get acquainted. We'll make friends eventually, like you and I did. We'll practically have to, being the only humans on the planet."

"No, Derec. We have to prove to him that we don't have a grudge—that people will help others just because they need it, and not because they're going to get something selfish out of it."

"Then let him prove it by helping you! You need to go worse than he does. That should be the basis for the decision."

"Maybe I shouldn't go, at least not yet."

"What? What do you mean, you shouldn't go?"

"Derec, I don't know where to look for a cure. I could just go out and wander, but that's not very reliable. Maybe if I stay here, Research 1 could take a culture from me and get to work on a cure. It might take a long time, but it would be a chance."

He hesitated, and looked at the unidentifiable equipment around the room. "The level of medical knowledge here is pretty erratic . . . but I guess the First Law might require him to try."

"And once that's set up, then I could take the next chance I had to leave."

"You could leave a culture with Research 1 now and go yourself."

"Leaving Jeff here that way just doesn't seem fair." She shook her head. "Besides, it would just help convince him that we're only out for ourselves."

"Is that the only reason?"

"Well, no." She looked away, smiling with embarrassment. "Anyway, why are you trying so hard to get rid of me?"

Derec folded his arms and shrugged. "Do you remember right after we first got here? I told you that I would stay to help the robots as they had asked, but that we could ask them to send you away."

"I told you I would stay with you." She nodded.

"Well, I've always been glad you decided to stay, but . . . I figure it would be better for you to go, that's all." He shrugged again, feeling his face grow hot.

"You want me to stay with you, don't you?" She had to bend

down a little to get under his lowered gaze, and she gave him a playful, knowing smile. "Don't you?"

"Well. . . ." He couldn't keep from smiling himself, but he was surprised when she put her arms around him and gave him a long hug. "As long as I'm still stuck here, anyhow. . . ." He had just recovered enough to hug her back when she patted him and pulled away.

She laughed. "Come on. Let's go tell him."

Jeff held the highly polished rectangle of metal in one hand and angled it so he could see himself. Research 1 had provided it in answer to his request for a mirror; the robots had not possessed, or ever desired, a personal mirror. He ran his hand along his jaw, then gently squeezed his cheeks so that his mouth puffed out. Then he smiled faintly at the face and wiggled his eyebrows up and down.

"It's you again," he said, almost in a whisper. "It's me again." He was losing the impulse to talk to himself, though, so he quit.

Still, he couldn't stop looking in his mirror. This was him, like he was supposed to be. He was back again. Jeff Leong, the eighteen-year-old, was alive and getting better, if not exactly well yet.

At the sound of a knock, he lowered the mirror. "Yeah?" He said quietly.

The door opened just enough for Ariel to stick her head inside. "We have to tell you something."

Jeff tensed. "Yeah?"

She and Derec entered the room. "We just wanted to let you know that as soon as you're well enough, we have a spacecraft that can take you off the planet. Depending on how fast you recover, you might still make the start of the new semester."

He studied their faces for a moment. "How much?"

Ariel looked at him, uncomprehending.

"It's free," said Derec.

"You're going to give me a spacecraft, supplies, and fuel for free? What do you want me to do for you?"

"Nothing!" Derec said angrily. "Listen, why—"

She stopped him with a hand on his arm. "Jeff, you can consider it a loan, if you like. As a matter of fact, if you could send someone back to pick us up someday—we don't have any money, either, and I know you don't—but if you ever got the chance to do that, it would be more than enough repayment."

"I'm no navigator," said Jeff. "I don't suppose I could send anyone back here, or even find it myself. I guess I should tell you that." He watched them closely, expecting them to change their minds.

"Fair enough," said Ariel. "We know that Mandelbrot lost his data when he stopped being Alpha, so he can't help, either."

Jeff shifted his gaze to Derec.

"When you're well enough, it's all yours." Derec nodded.

Jeff looked at them both without speaking, not sure whether to believe them or not. From the moment he had first awakened on this planet, virtually nothing that he had seen, heard, or done had been believable. This was no different.

"Did you hear what we said?" Ariel asked.

"Yeah." His voice was low and wary.

They looked at each other uncertainly. He watched them, not sure what to expect. Then, without further comment, they left.

Jeff's physical recovery progressed well, and Derec suspected that the First Law made his robot medical team more cautious and conservative in their judgments than human doctors would have been. Still, even when it was clear that his brain had been successfully transplanted, his bodily injuries also had to heal. He remained quiet and wary in his manner, but he was no longer egotistical or insulting. Ariel noticed that that behavior had vanished with his robot body.

Derec suggested to Ariel that they form a farewell gathering for Jeff's lift-off. Once he had recovered enough to travel, Mandelbrot set the computer in the little ship and gave him a quick course in its manual controls, in the event of emergency. Basically, the computer was to locate the nearest spacelane and wait there, sending a continuous distress signal. No one, including the robots, questioned that in a major spacelane he would be picked up before his life-support ran out.

Jeff remained quiet and cautious even as he was about to leave, but Research 1 was certain that the physical effects of his experience were wearing off.

"He has been integrated with his body for some time now,"

said Research 1. "His serum levels are his own."

As they stood near the hangar waiting for Jeff to enter the ship, Ariel added, "After he's back in normal human society again, I'm sure he'll be okay."

"He hasn't acted very grateful," said Derec. "After all, we don't have to send him. Both of us want to get out of here, too."

"Shh," said Ariel.

Jeff walked up to them. He still moved slowly and tentatively sometimes, but he was fully mobile now. "I just wanted to tell you that if I can figure out where this planet is, I'll get word to some emergency people."

"I know you will," said Ariel. "Have a good trip."

"And thanks for the, uh, chance to go." He looked away shyly.

"It's all right," said Derec. "Take care of yourself."

Jeff looked up at Research 1 and Surgeon 1 with a slight grin. "Well, it's certainly been interesting knowing you two. Thanks for getting me all back together."

"You are welcome," they said in unison.

He looked around at them all, and stopped at Wolruf. "You okay, kiddo?"

"Okay," said Wolruf, with a furry nod that quivered her pointed ears. "'U be careful on 'urr trip."

"Well . . . good-bye." Jeff nodded awkwardly and joined Mandelbrot at the ship. The robot would make sure he was properly prepared for lift-off.

Moments later, he was in the ship and it was roaring away, ascending quickly into the sky until it was only a sliver of light reflected from the sun.

Derec watched it rise, squinting into the deep sky until the back of his neck hurt from the strain. "Our one greatest wish," he said. "And we gave it away."

Ariel took his arm in both her hands and leaned against him. "We did right, Derec. Besides, we aren't through yet."

He looked down at her and grinned. "Not us—not by a long shot."

Together, they turned and led the little group back toward Robot City.

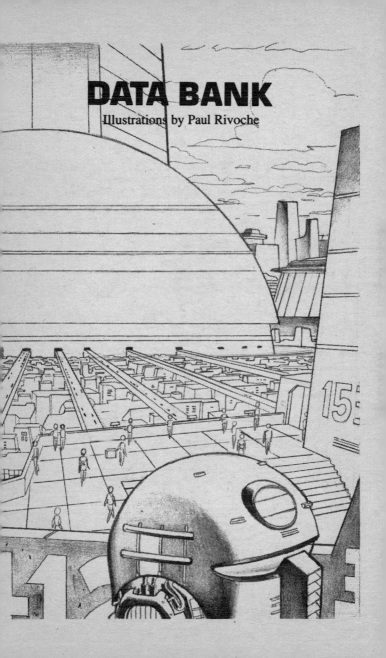

DATA BANK

Illustrations by Paul Rivoche

THE KEY CENTER: The Key Center is a great bronze-colored dome constructed of dianite. It houses facilities for analysis, construction, initializing, and storage of duplicate Keys to Perihelion. This is a totally new structure, built after the uncontrolled growth of Robot City was slowed, and the original Key had been taken from its hiding place on the Compass Tower by the robots.

The final phase of initializing the keys takes place on the second floor. The last stage of actual construction involves developing the individual key's fifth dimension.

As the key's fifth dimension is attached during construction, however, an opening into hyperspace occurs within the construction equipment. This draws in air, creating an extremely powerful vacuum effect in Robot City. This vacuum side effect is harnessed by the Vacuum Tube Small Cargo System, keeping such a powerful energy source from going to waste.

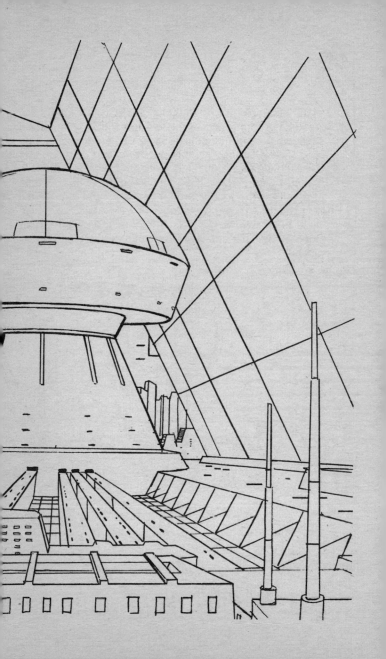

THE VACUUM TUBE SMALL CARGO TRANSPORT
SYSTEM: The vacuum system is actually based on
twentieth-century technology; the engineers of Robot City
have merely refined its efficiency to a very high degree.
Air is drawn to a central hub underground, below the Key
Center, by the powerful suction created in the initialization
of duplicate Keys to Perihelion on the second floor of the
Key Center. A complex system of tubes, carefully mea-
sured in its ascents, descents, and curves, runs throughout
Robot City, sometimes overground, sometimes underground.

The vacuum propels the transparent cargo modules through the transparent chutes. The modules' interiors are three meters long by two meters wide and are padded and ventilated sufficiently to allow humans to be transported within them safely.

At each stop, sidings allow individual containers to be routed out of the main line by computer, carried by their forward momentum into the loading area. After loading or unloading, a small roller underneath the container then carries it through an irised door back into the trunk line of the vacuum tube.

THE TUNNEL TRANSPORTATION SYSTEM: The Tunnel Transportation System is designed exclusively for humans and humanoid robots. Like the vacuum cargo system, it was constructed after the uncontrolled growth of Robot City ceased.

Individual platform booths have consoles that can receive the rider's destination through either a robotic comlink or a voice command. Function robots, lacking positronic brains, cannot utilize the platforms. The booths are built around the platforms as windshields, so that the platforms can travel at a speed that would otherwise push the riders off.

The platforms travel on multiple tracks that run parallel and occasionally branch off or merge together. All the destinations go into the tunnel computer, which then organizes the route and speed of each platform to maximize the efficiency of the entire system.

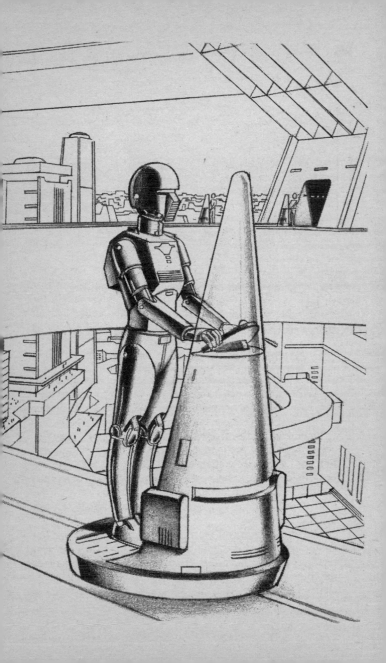

DIANITE: Dianite is an advanced form of the substance from which most of Robot City is constructed. It is extremely thin and light, with high tensile strength. Individual cells of dianite are shaped like tiny Keys to Perihelion. Each cell of dianite has very strong filaments that cross inside the cell and terminate at each corner. When one cell bonds to another, the corners, or angles, that bond create a particularly strong link at the interface of the two filaments. This creates a stiffening effect that increases as more corners of the cells bond to each other. When a cell is fully bonded on every face and angle, its position is firmly fixed and the result is a hard, stiff substance. However, the uneven shape of the cells means that when some of the faces are unbonded, the existing bonds are vulnerable to slight pressure. That is why a tear, once begun, is easy to continue. The fine textured surface of dianite is also caused by the uneven shape of the cells.

Dianite is strongest in a straight, flat sheet, unlike some other substances. The shape of the cells is such that curving, as in a dome or in corrugation, lowers the number of angles and faces on each cell that actually bond with other cells. The dome of the Key Center is constructed of a double thickness of dianite. The interface of the two domed sheets that are layered together increases the number of bonded angles and faces, thereby strengthening the dome.

THE CYBORG: To all external appearances, the robot body into which Jeff Leong's brain is transplanted is identical to those of many other robots in Robot City. It is a model selected for its adaptability to human needs—stereoptic vision and stereophonic hearing, for example—but is still one of the standard models.

This particular robot body was adapted by removing the positronic brain and strengthening the brain case to protect Jeff's human brain. Neuroelectronic connectors were then set in place to give the brain control over the body, and receptacles of highly concentrated nutrients and hormones were set into the lower part of the head and the upper part of the neck, with a metered system to provide enough food to keep the brain alive.

Insufficient knowledge of the proper physiochemical balances by the robot surgeons led to Jeff's mental problems; otherwise the surgery was a complete success.

WILLIAM F. WU

William F. Wu is a five-time nominee for the Hugo, Nebula, and World Fantasy Awards. He is the author of the novel *MasterPlay*, about computer wargamers for hire, and he has had short fiction published in most of the magazines and many anthologies in the field of science fiction and fantasy, including a series of collaborations with Rob Chilson in *Analog*. His short story, "Wong's Lost and Found Emporium," was adapted into an episode of the new *Twilight Zone* television show in 1985 and his first published story, "By the Flicker of the One-Eyed Flame," was adapted and performed on stage in 1977. He holds a Ph.D. in American Culture from the University of Michigan, and is married to fantasy artist Diana Gallagher Wu.

BESTSELLING
Science Fiction
and
Fantasy